W8-CDQ-982

Mother was sitting in her green stuffed rocking chair when I walked through the door. "You can turn around and walk right out. I know everything that went on up there, the dean of women called me up. You just turn your ass around and get out."

"Mom, you only know what they told you."

"I know you let your ass run away with your head, that's what I know. A queer, I raised a queer, that's what I know. You're lower than them dirty fruit pickers in the groves, you know that?"

"Mom, you don't understand anything. Why don't you let me tell my side of it?"

"I don't want to hear nothing you can say. You always were a bad one. Go on and get outa here. I don't want you. Why the hell you even bother to come back here?"

"Because you're the only family I got. Where else am I gonna go?"

"That's your problem, smart-pants. You'll have no friends and you got no family. Let's see how far you get, you little snot-nose. You thought you'd go to college and be better than me. You thought you'd go mix with the rich. And you still think you're dandy, don't you? Even being a stinking queer don't shake you none. Well, I hope I live to see the day you put your tail between your legs. I'll laugh right in your face."

"Then you'd better live to see me dead." I picked up my suitcase by the door and walked out into the cool night air. I had $14.61 in my jeans. That wouldn't get me half to New York City. And that's where I was going. There are so many queers in New York that one more wouldn't rock the boat.

Rubyfruit Jungle

RITA MAE BROWN

BANTAM BOOKS
NEW YORK • TORONTO • LONDON • SYDNEY • AUCKLAND

This edition contains the complete text of the original hardcover edition.
NOT ONE WORD HAS BEEN OMITTED.

RUBYFRUIT JUNGLE
A Bantam Book / published by arrangement with the author

PUBLISHING HISTORY
Daughters Publishing Company edition published 1973
Bantam edition / September 1977
Parts of this book have appeared in the AMAZON QUARTERLY

ISBN 0-553-27886-X

Published simultaneously in the United States and Canada

Bantam Books are published by Bantam Books, a division of Bantam Doubleday Dell
Publishing Group, Inc. Its trademark, consisting of the words "Bantam Books" and the
portrayal of a rooster, is Registered in U.S. Patent and Trademark Office and in other
countries. Marca Registrada. Bantam Books, 1540 Broadway, New York, New York 10036.

PRINTED IN THE UNITED STATES OF AMERICA

RAD 40 39 38 37 36 35 34 33

Dedicated to
ALEXIS SMITH

Actress, Wit, Beauty, Cook, Kindheart, Irreverent Observer of Political Phenomena, Etc. If I were to list her outstanding qualities, you, dear reader, would be exhausted before you get to page one. So let me just say the abovementioned woman took the time to give me a playful push in the direction of my typewriter. Of course, after you read the book, you may wish that she had pushed me in front of something moving faster than a typewriter.

Acknowledgments

Thank you to Charlotte Bunch for helping me win one year's fellowship at the Institute for Policy Studies in Washington, D.C. The job allowed me the time to write this book. Thank you to Frances Chapman and Onka Dekkers who read an unpunctuated mess and untangled it. And thank you to Tasha Burd for sticking it out with me when I was alone.

No one remembers her beginnings. Mothers and aunts tell us about infancy and early childhood, hoping we won't forget the past when they had total control over our lives and secretly praying that because of it, we'll include them in our future.

I didn't know anything about my own beginnings until I was seven years old, living in Coffee Hollow, a rural dot outside of York, Pennsylvania. A dirt road connected tarpapered houses filled with smear-faced kids and the air was always thick with the smell of coffee beans freshly ground in the small shop that gave the place its name. One of those smear-faced kids was Brockhurst Detwiler, Broccoli for short. It was through him that I learned I was a bastard. Broccoli didn't know I was a bastard but he and I struck a bargain that cost me my ignorance.

One crisp September day Broccoli and I were

on our way home from Violet Hill Elementary School.

"Hey, Molly, I gotta take a leak, wanna see me?"

"Sure, Broc."

He stepped behind the bushes and pulled down his zipper with a flourish.

"Broccoli, what's all that skin hanging around your dick?"

"My mom says I haven't had it cut up yet."

"Whaddaya mean, cut up?"

"She says that some people get this operation and the skin comes off and it has somethin' to do with Jesus."

"Well, I'm glad no one's gonna cut up on me."

"That's what you think. My Aunt Louise got her tit cut off."

"I ain't got tits."

"You will. You'll get big floppy ones just like my mom. They hang down below her waist and wobble when she walks."

"Not me, I ain't gonna look like that."

"Oh yes you are. All girls look like that."

"You shut up or I'll knock your lips down your throat, Broccoli Detwiler."

"I'll shut up if you don't tell anyone I showed you my thing."

"What's there to tell? All you got is a wad of pink wrinkles hangin' around it. It's ugly."

"It is not ugly."

"Ha. It looks awful. You think it's not ugly because it's yours. No one else has a dick like that. My cousin Leroy, Ted, no one. I bet you got the only one in the world. We oughta make some money off it."

4

"Money? How we gonna make money off my dick?"

"After school we can take the kids back here and show you off, and we charge a nickel a piece."

"No. I ain't showing people my thing if they're gonna laugh at it."

"Look, Broc, money is money. What do you care if they laugh? You'll have money then you can laugh at them. And we split it fifty-fifty."

The next day during recess I spread the news. Broccoli was keeping his mouth shut. I was afraid he'd chicken out but he came through. After school about eleven of us hurried out to the woods between school and the coffee shop and there Broc revealed himself. He was a big hit. Most of the girls had never even seen a regular dick and Broccoli's was so disgusting they shrieked with pleasure. Broc looked a little green around the edges, but he bravely kept it hanging out until everyone had a good look. We were fifty-five cents richer.

Word spread through the other grades, and for about a week after that, Broccoli and I had a thriving business. I bought red licorice and handed it out to all my friends. Money was power. The more red licorice you had, the more friends you had. Leroy, my cousin, tried to horn in on the business by showing himself off, but he flopped because he didn't have skin on him. To make him feel better, I gave him fifteen cents out of every day's earnings.

Nancy Cahill came every day after school to look at Broccoli, billed as the "strangest dick in the world." Once she waited until everyone else had left. Nancy was all freckles and rosary beads.

She giggled every time she saw Broccoli and on that day she asked if she could touch him. Broccoli stupidly said yes. Nancy grabbed him and gave a squeal..

"Okay, okay, Nancy, that's enough. You might wear him out and we have other customers to satisfy." That took the wind out of her and she went home. "Look, Broccoli, what's the big idea of letting Nancy touch you for free? That ought to be worth at least a dime. We oughta let kids do it for a dime and Nancy can play for free when everyone goes home if you want her to."

"Deal."

This new twist drew half the school into the woods. Everything was fine until Earl Stambach ratted on us to Miss Martin, the teacher. Miss Martin contacted Carrie and Broccoli's mother and it was all over.

When I got home that night I didn't even get through the door when Carrie yells, "Molly, come in here right this minute." The tone in her voice told me I was up for getting strapped.

"I'm coming, Mom."

"What's this I hear about you out in the woods playing with Brockhurst Detwiler's peter? Don't lie to me now, Earl told Miss Martin you're out there every night."

"Not me, Mom, I never played with him." Which was true.

"Don't lie to me, you big-mouthed brat. I know you were out there jerking that dimwit off. And in front of all the other brats in the Hollow."

"No, Mom, honest, I didn't do that." There was no use telling her what I really did. She wouldn't have believed me. Carrie assumed all children lied.

6

"You shamed me in front of all the neighbors, and I've got a good mind to throw you outa this house. You and your high and mighty ways, sailing in the house and out the house as you damn well please. You reading them books and puttin' on airs. You're a fine one to be snotty Miss Ups, out there in the woods playing with his old dong. Well, I got news for you, you little shitass, you think you're so smart. You ain't so fine as you think you are, and you ain't mine neither. And I don't want you now that I know what you're about. Wanna know who you are, smartypants? You're Ruby Drollinger's bastard, that's who you are. Now let's see you put your nose in the air."

"Who's Ruby Drollinger?"

"Your real mother, that's who and she was a slut, you hear me, Miss Molly? A common, dirty slut who'd lay with a dog if it shook its ass right."

"I don't care. It makes no difference where I came from. I'm here, ain't I?"

"It makes all the difference in the world. Them that's born in wedlock are blessed by the Lord. Them that's born out of wedlock are cursed as bastards. So there."

"I don't care."

"Well, you oughta care, you horse's ass. Just see how far all your pretty ways and books get you when you go out and people find out you're a bastard. And you act like one Blood's thicker than water and yours tells. Bullheaded like Ruby and out there in the woods jerking off that Detwiler idiot. Bastard!"

Carrie was red in the face and her veins were popping out of her neck. She looked like a one-woman horror movie and she was thumping the

7

table and thumping me. She grabbed me by the shoulders and shook me like a dog shakes a rag doll. "Snot-nosed, bitch of a bastard. Living in my house, under my roof. You'd be dead in that orphanage if I hadn't gotten you out and nursed you round the clock. You come here and eat the food, keep me runnin' after you and then go out and shame me. You better straighten up, girl, or I'll throw you back where you came from—the gutter."

"Take your hands off me. If you ain't my real mother then you just take your goddamned hands off me." I ran out the door and tore all the way over the wheat fields up to the woods. The sun had gone down, and there was one finger of rose left in the sky.

So what, so what I'm a bastard. I don't care. She's trying to scare me. She's always trying to throw some fear in me. The hell with her and the hell with anyone else if it makes a difference to them. Goddamn Broccoli Detwiler and his ugly dick anyway. He got me in this mess and just when we're making money this has to happen. I'm gonna get Earl Stambach and lay him out to whaleshit if it's the last thing I do. Yeah, then Mom will rip me for that. I wonder who else knows I'm a bastard. I bet Mouth knows and if Florence the Megaphone Mouth knows, the whole world knows. I bet they're all sittin' on it like hens. Well, I ain't going back into that house for them to laugh at me and look at me like I'm a freak. I'm staying out here in these woods and I'm gonna kill Earl. Shit, I wonder if ole Broc got it. He'll tell I put him up to it and skin out. Coward. Anyone with a dick like that's gotta be chickenshit any-

way. I wonder if any of the kids know. I can face
Mouth and Mom but not the gang. Well, if it
makes a difference to them, the hell with them,
too. I can't see why it's such a big deal. Who cares
how you get here? I don't care. I really don't care.
I got myself born, that's what counts. I'm here.
Boy, ole Mom was really roaring, she was ripped,
just ripped. I'm not going back there. I'm not
going back to where it makes a difference and
she'll throw it in my face from now on out. Look
how she throws in my face how I kicked Grandma
Bolt's shins when I was five. I'm staying in these
woods. I can live off nuts and berries, except I
don't like berries, they got ticks on them. I can
just live off nuts, I guess. Maybe kill rabbits, yeah,
but Ted told me rabbits are full of worms. Worms,
yuk, I'm not eating worms. I'll stay out here in
these woods and starve, that's what I'll do. Then
Mom will feel sorry about how she yelled at me
and made a big deal out of the way I was born.
And calling my real mother a slut—I wonder
what my real mother looks like. Maybe I look like
someone. I don't look like anyone in our house,
none of the Bolts nor Wiegenlieds, none of them.
They all have extra white skin and gray eyes.
German, they're all German. And don't Carrie
make noise about that. How anyone else is bad,
Wops and Jews and the rest of the entire world.
That's why she hates me. I bet my mother wasn't
German. My mother couldn't have cared about
me very much if she left me with Carrie. Did I do
something wrong way back then? Why would she
leave me like that? Now, maybe now she could
leave me after showing off Broccoli's dick but
when I was a little baby how could I have done

9

anything wrong? I wish I'd never heard any of this. I wish Carrie Bolt would drop down dead. That's exactly what I wish. I'm not going back there.

Night drew around the woods and little unseen animals burrowed in the dark. There was no moon. The black filled my nostrils and the air was full of little noises, weird sounds. A chill came up off the old fishpond down by the pine trees. I couldn't find any nuts either, it was too dark. All I found was a spider's nest. The spider's nest did it. I decided to go back to the house but only until I was old enough to get a job so I could leave that dump. Stumbling, I felt my way home and opened the torn screen door. No one was waiting up for me. They'd all gone to bed.

Leroy sat in the middle of the potato patch picking a tick off his navel. He looked like Baby Huey in the comics and he was about as smart, but Leroy was my cousin and in a dumb way I loved him. We'd been sent out there to get potato bugs, but the sun was high and we were both tired of our chores. The grown-up women were in the house, and the men were off working. That was the summer of 1956, and we were in such bad shape that we had to live with the Denmans in Shiloh. I didn't know we were in bad shape; besides I liked being out there with Leroy, Ted and all the animals.

Leroy was eleven, same age as me. He was the same height only fat; I was skinny. Ted, Leroy's brother, was thirteen and his voice was changing. Ted worked down at the Esso station so Leroy and I were stuck with the potato bugs.

"Molly, I don't wanna pick bugs no more. We got two jars full, let's go on down to Mrs. Hershener's and get a soda."

"Okay, but we got to go down by the gully where Ted wrecked the tractor or my mom will see us and make us get back to work." We crawled through the gully, past the rusty tractor and out the drainpipe to the other side of the dirt road. Then we ran all the way down to Mrs. Hershener's tiny store which had a faded Nehi soda sign with a thermometer on it tacked to the door.

"Well, it's Leroy and Molly. You children been helping your mothers up there on the hill?"

"Oh yes, Mrs. Hershener," Leroy droned, "we spent this whole day picking potato bugs so the potatoes will grow right."

"Now aren't you just sweet. Here, how about a chocolate Tastycake for each of you."

"Thank you, Mrs. Hershener"—in unison.

"Can I get a scoop of raspberry ice cream for a nickel?" I grabbed my ice cream and walked out into the June sunshine. Leroy strolled out with a fudge ripple and we sat on the worn, flat wood planks of the porch. I spied an empty Sunmaid raisin box, nearly perfect except the top was torn, lying there in the irridescent tarpaper shavings in front of the store.

"What you want that for?"

"I got plans for this, you wait and see."

"Come on, Moll, tell me and I'll help you."

"Can't tell you now, here comes Barbara Spangenthau and you know how she is."

"Yeah, right, gotta be a secret."

"Hi, Barbara, watchyou doin?"

Barbara mumbled something about a loaf of

bread and disappeared inside. Barbara was Jewish and Carrie was forever telling Leroy and me to keep away from her. She needn't have bothered. No one wanted to go near Barbara Spangenthau because she always had her hand in her pants playing with herself and worse, she stank. Until I was fifteen I thought that being Jewish meant you walked around with your hand in your pants.

Barbara rolled out of the store. She was even fatter than Leroy; her arms full of Fishel's bread, she started down the footpath with all the honey-suckles.

"Hey Barbara, you seen Earl Stambach today?"

"He was down by the pond. Why?"

"Cause I got a present for him. You see him you tell him I'm lookin' for him, hear?"

Barbara, filled with importance of her message, trotted down the road. Since she lived closest to the Stambachs, there was a good chance she'd deliver it.

"What you want to give Earl Stambach a present for? I thought you hated him since forever."

"I do hate him, and the present I got for him is something very special. You want to come with me while I get it?"

Leroy fell over himself in enthusiasm, and he trailed me back over the fields like a duck after its mother, all the way babbling about what the present's gonna be. We went into the cool woods and I searched the ground. Leroy was looking at the ground too, although he didn't know what he was looking for.

"Ha! I got it. Now I'm gonna fix him good."

"I don't see nothin' but a pile of rabbit turds. What you gonna do? Come on and tell."

"Just watch, Leroy, and shut your trap."

I scooped up a handful of tiny, perfectly round rabbit turds and put them in the Sunmaid raisin box.

"Remember the dried raisins that Florence had out on the back porch? You go on down there and steal me a handful and come right back here."

Leroy took off like a cement truck, his bulk shimmering in the afternoon sun. Within ten minutes he was back with a precious handful of honest raisins. I put them in the box and shook the contents hard. Then swearing Leroy to eternal secrecy, I started through the woods to Carmine's fishpond to find Earl Stambach. He was down there all right, sitting there with a stick for a fishing pole waiting for nonexistent fish to bite a string with no bait on it. Earl was pretty stupid. The only way he made it through fourth grade was by brownnosing the teacher. We were now going into sixth grade and he still couldn't get beyond five on the multiplication tables. Florence said it was because the Stambachs had so many kids that none of them ate enough, so Earl's brain was starved. I didn't much care why he was stupid, I was too busy hating him. He was all the time ratting on me in school because I was breaking this rule or that rule. Last time, I was sent to Mr. Beaver's office for stealing tablets out of the supply room. That was one week before school ended and I nearly didn't get out of fifth grade because of it. Earl might be stupid but he learned how to survive and he learned at my expense, the mealymouthed weasel.

Earl heard us coming and looked up. A perplexed shadow ran across his face because he must have thought I was going to whip him for sure. So I smiled and said, "Hey, Earl, hey, you catching anything?"

"No, but I got a big bite just five minutes ago. It must have been a tuna because it was sure big."

"Zat so? You must be a talented fisherman."

Earl giggled and his left eye twitched. He couldn't figure this no way.

"Earl, I been thinkin' that we got to stop irritatin' each other. Now you know I hate it when you stool on me, and I know you hate it when I get mad at you and lay for you on your way home from school. Why don't we call a truce and be friends? I won't beat you up if you don't tell on me when we go back to school."

"Sure, Molly, sure. I'd like us to be friends and I swear on a stack of Bibles I won't tell on you ever again."

"Well, here then, I brought you a little present to make it legal. I just got them at Mrs. Hersh-ener's cause I know you love raisins."

"Thanks, hey thanks." Earl snatched the raisin box, tore off what was left of the top and opened his mouth, tipped the box over it and gulped half the contents in one motion. Leroy started to laugh. I grabbed his left arm and gave him a pinch that would have ruined an orange, "You hush your mouth or I'll whip your ass," I hissed.

"I ain't worried, Molly, I ain't gonna laugh."

"What you two talking about?"

"Oh, we was remarking how fast you eat, Earl. We ain't never seen anyone eat quite so fast. Why you must be the fastest eater in all of York County. I bet you can finish off the rest of the box in half a second. Don't you think so, Leroy?"

"Yeah, Earl Stambach has got true speed. He even eats faster than my old man."

Earl bloated up with all this praise, and he ruffled out his feathers. "Oh, I can do it in less than half a second, you watch me." One fierce swallow and the Sunmaid raisin box was tossed into the pond. Earl was beaming and feeling big on himself.

"Earl, how did those raisins taste?"

"Like raisins, some were mushy and bitter though."

"Mushy, now ain't that the strangest thing?"

Leroy exploded with laughter and fell down on the grass next to the pond. "Earl, you are so stupid. You know that, Earl, you are so stupid. Molly gave you a box full of rabbit turds mixed with raisins."

Earl's face crumpled under the blow. "You didn't do that, did you, Molly?"

"You bet I did, you sneaking fart. You rat on me one more time and I'm gonna do a whole lot worse so you'd better lay off me, Earl Stambach. Let this be a lesson to you." I took a threatening step toward him for effect but Earl was so green he wasn't worried about the outside of his body. "I won't ever tell on you again. I promise, I promise. Cross my heart and hope to die."

" 'Die' is the right word, boy. You button your fat lip and if you even breathe a single word that I fed you rabbit turds, you've had it. Come on, Leroy, let's leave him here full of shit."

We scurried over the pine needles and Leroy was laughing so hard he could barely keep his footing. I turned around on the rim of the hill to look at Earl down by the edge of the pond retching his guts out and crying at the same time. Fixed him good, I thought, I fixed him real good and he deserves it. How come I don't feel good about it?

"He ain't gonna bother you no more, Molly, you got him this time."

"Shut up, Leroy, you shut up."

Leroy stopped for a minute and looked at me with amazement, then shrugged his shoulders and said, "We better get on back home before Carrie and the Mouth come looking for us."

3

The summer of my revenge was also the summer that the crops died and Jennifer died too. Jennifer was Leroy's real mother. She was tall with a face like those ladies in Sunday School books. Her eyes were so big that when you looked at her that's all you could see. I called her Aunt Jenna although she wasn't really my aunt, but then none of them were my family. That summer was full of bad things, and it started with Ep's getting trimmed with a knife.

Couple of days after I got Earl good, Ep, Jennifer's husband, came in the house covered with blood. It ran down his face and matted in the thick, curly, blond hair on his huge chest. Jennifer screamed when she saw him, and Florence ran to the kitchen for a bowl of cold water. For all her faults, Florence was always the first to grasp what was needed in any situation. My dad

Carl hadn't come home yet so just us kids and the women were there—with Ep soaking in blood and looking so mad I thought his brains would fry. Leroy's eyes almost fell out of his head when he looked at his old man all busted up. Ep didn't notice the two of us standing there, staring. Ted eased his father down into a chair and Florence came back into the room with basin, rags and an air of command. "Put your head back, Ep, and let me get the blood off your face. Molly, go in the pantry and get gauze and merthiolate. Leroy, go pump more water for your father. Jennifer, you sit down, you lookin' pale as a ghost. Now, Ep, hold still. I know it hurts, but you just hold still. It ain't gonna hurt nearly as bad as when you got stuck in the first place."

Ep gave in and let his head hang back, wincing each time the rag touched his wounds. He didn't get busted, he got carved. "Ep," Jennifer said low, "honey, what happened? You went and lost your temper again, didn't you?"

Ep's anger started to drain away and he answered quietly, "Yes, I went and lost my head but I couldn't help it and I didn't have one drink, I swear, not one drink."

Florence gave him a dirty look but kept on with her business. "Molly, go over to your Aunt Jenna and get her to show you how to make a butterfly stitch out of adhesive tape. Make a lot, he's got holes in him big as mouths."

Leroy padded back into the room and sat a bowl of water on the oil tablecloth. "Hey, Pop, you get him, the guy that got you? You get him, Pop?"

"Leroy, I wish you wouldn't ask those questions with such joy in your face," Jennifer pleaded. She looked old, so old sometimes, and this was one of those times. The color seemed to have left her face and hidden somewhere. The lines around the top of her upper lip were drawn and it made her look strange. She was about two weeks away from having another baby. She looked like a grandmother that swallowed a weather balloon, and Carrie said that Jennifer was only thirty-three years old.

"What was the fight about this time?" she asked.

"Fought about the boys with that bastard, Layton." That word made me cringe. How come whenever a person was bad they called him a bastard? My face went hot and I didn't dare look up from my butterfly bandages for fear someone would see my color. "Layton he come on into the shop all puffed up like a banty rooster about his son, Phil. Phil got an appointment to West Point he says; then he gives me this sly look and asks how my boys doing. Well, I told him both Ted and Leroy going to the Point too. After all, I'm a veteran, got a purple heart and they ain't gonna refuse my boys when they are ready to go. They can't turn away sons of men shot up in the war. So Layton he roars laughing and says that being the son of a fool got shot up in the war don't mean they can go to so high a place as West Point. He says everyone on the hill knows my boys are so dumb they don't know their ass from their elbow. Well Jenna, I couldn't stand it no more. I told him his son Phil don't deserve to belong to the army, that pansy sits down to piss . . . we got into it after that and I laid him to whaleshit. Then he pulls a toadsticker on me and well, there's not more to tell."

"There's a lot more to tell," Florence intervened. "The cops gonna come down here and haul you off if you gonna get in fights like trash. How'd you leave Layton? You didn't kill him, I hope?"

"Nah, I didn't kill him though I'd have liked to wrung his neck until his tongue hit the ground. Carl came by the shop on his way home and broke it up. He's down there now making some kind of peace with Layton. You know Carl's so good-natured he can get anyone feeling good again. He sent me home because I wasn't any help."

Jennifer got up to check the snap beans cooking on the stove. Ep looked at the floor and studied his dusty shoes. "Honey," he called out, "our boys ain't stupid. They'll do good, you wait. Seeing them do good will make me feel better than pounding on Layton anyway."

Jennifer turned from the bubbling water and walked back in the room to give him a kiss. "Sure, they'll do all right, but I don't think fighting is an example for them." A sheepish grin took over Ep's face, and he put his hand on her bloated belly and kissed her hand.

Carl came through the door and made a big show out of tossing his gray worker's cap on the coat rack. He made it and we all gave a cheer. Under his arm he had a big piece of meat wrapped in greasy butcher's paper. His gold tooth in front glittered as he smiled. "Lamb stew tonight, folks. It was left over after the day and I brought it home. So get out the carrots and celery, we're gonna have lamb stew." Carrie sidled over to Carl and whispered in his ear. He patted her on the shoulder and told her everything was fine.

I ran over and jumped up high to put my arms

around his neck. "Come on, Daddy, swing me in a circle till I get dizzy."

"All right, pilot to copilot, here we go–o–o." Carl worked hard and his robust, muscular body already had a taint of early age about it, different from Jennifer's but bowed some way.

After my swing, he went over to Ep and asked him how he was doing. Ep looked up to Carl the way boys look up to their fathers even though Carl was only ten years older than Ep.

"Supper's on the way, gang. Clear off this table and get these bloody rags out of the way," Carrie announced later. The stew was brought steaming to the table and Leroy and I fought for a place next to Carl. Jennifer and Ep kept looking at each other over the table and Florence ran her mouth more than usual but there was no edge in her voice this time. She wanted to smooth things out. Leroy forgot to steal meat off my plate and Carrie laughed at everything Carl said. Carl talked more than I remembered him ever doing. He told stories about Sure Mike the burly man he worked for at the butcher shop, and he joked about the president of the United States. The grownups laughed at those jokes more than anything but they didn't make sense to me. In school they told us that the president was the best man in the whole country but I knew my father was the best man in the whole country; the country didn't know it, that's all. So I guessed it was okay for Carl to make fun of the president. Anyway, how did I know the president was for real? I never saw him, just pictures in the paper and they can make those up. How do you know someone is real if you don't see him?

Jennifer was losing weight instead of gaining it like you're supposed to do when you have a baby but she was so close to having the baby that no one paid much attention except Carrie. When it came time for Jennifer to go to the George Street Hospital, things seemed regular enough She had the baby, named Carl after Dad, but the baby only lived two days. She didn't come home. The grownups paid less attention to us than usual. Coming in from the outhouse, I stopped on the porch and heard Florence, Carrie, and Ep. It was a hot, sticky night. Leroy was on the porch spitting watermelon seeds, so we both sat and listened.

Ep's voice sounded like a fuzzy radio show. He sounded worse than when he got cut up. "Carrie, she never told me about no pains. She never told me anything. If she'd let me know how she was feeling, I'd have got her to a doctor."

Florence answered him in a calm voice that was even stern, "My daughter, Jennifer, never was one to put herself first. She figured doctors ran too high and whatever was the matter with her had to do with the baby, so it'd be soon gone. Don't blame yourself, Ep. She did what she thought was right and God knows with all of us working we can't make hardly enough to keep going. She was thinking about that."

"I'm her husband. She should have told me. It's my duty to know."

Carrie came in on it. "Women often get ailments they keep from their men. Jennifer was quieter than most that way. She mentioned to me that she had pains but how were any of us to know she's shot through with cancer? She didn't know. You don't know things like that."

"She's going to die. I know she's going to die. When it's all through you like that, you can't live."

"No, there's no way she can live. These things are in the hands of the Lord." Florence was resolute. Fate was fate. If God wanted Jennifer then he would have her. Carrie seconded the motion. " 'The Lord giveth and the Lord taketh away.' It's not our business, these things, birth and death. We have to keep going on."

Leroy looked at me and clutched my arm. "Molly, Molly what does it mean that Mom's got cancer? What are they talking about? Tell me what they're talking about."

"I don't know, Leroy. They say Aunt Jenna's gonna die." My throat hurt, there was a burning lump in it and I held onto Leroy's hand and whispered, "Don't let them know we heard. Nothin' we can do except stay out of their way and see what happens. Maybe it's a mistake and she'll be home soon. People make mistakes sometimes." Leroy started to cry and I took him out by the lima beans so nobody would hear either of us. Leroy sobbed, "I don't want my mom to die." He cried himself sick and then fell asleep. Even the mosquitoes didn't bother him. After awhile Carrie called us to come in, so I got him up and half carried fat, lumpy Leroy back to the house to his little iron bed. Leroy slept in the same room with Ted, and I slept with Carrie and Carl in my own bed. I'd rather have been in there with Leroy, but people said it wasn't right, but that made no sense to me at all, especially tonight. "Mom, let me stay in here with Leroy, just for tonight, Mom, please?"

"No, you're not sleeping in here with the boys

and Ted big enough so his voice is changing. You come where you belong. When you get older you'll understand." She hauled me off and I took one last look at poor Leroy, eyes red and swollen and groggy. He was too tired to protest and fell back into a stupor.

He must have told Ted because next day Ted was more withdrawn than usual and his eyes looked red too.

Within a week Jenna was gone. The funeral was jammed with the entire population of the Hollow, and people were impressed with the flowers. Ep busted himself on the casket. He got the best there was and nobody could talk him out of it. If his wife was going to be dead, then she was going to be dead right, he said. Florence took charge of everything. Leroy, Ted and I were banished during the preparations and that was fine with us. Everybody got all dressed up to honor the dead. Leroy wore a bow tie, Ted wore a string tie, and Daddy and Ep had long ties on and coats that didn't match their trousers, but coats just the same. Carrie rigged me in a horrible dress full of itchy crinolines and patent leather shoes. At least Jennifer was beyond being tormented by itchy dresses. I thought I was worse off than the corpse. The service went on and on, the preacher got carried away with himself over the casket as he talked about the joys of heaven. When they lowered the gleaming box into the ground, Florence swooned and gasped, "My baby." Carl grabbed her and held her up. Ep had Ted and Leroy by the hand, and he never moved a muscle. He stared straight into that hole and never said a word. Leroy was trying hard not to start bawling again, and I stared at the cowlick on back of his slicked-down hair so as not to start crying myself and show up for a big sissy. The dress didn't help none, it's easier to cry in a dress anyway.

After the casket was in the ground we all went back to the house. Neighbors and relatives from as far away as Harrisburg had come and they brought food. I don't know why, because no one felt like eating. Ep received people with a pained dignity and Florence almost enjoyed the attention she was getting as mother of the deceased but it was mixed with sorrow. So much of what Florence did was mixed that way.

Once it got dark, people started to clear out and finally we were left to ourselves. Carrie set the table to try to get us kids to eat. Carl passed the fruit bread and put a hunk on my plate. "The candied cherries are cut up in little red pieces. Take a bite, it's real good."

"I don't wanna eat, Daddy. I'm not hungry." I pushed the food around on my plate to make it look as though I'd had some. After a proper amount of time the table was cleared and we went off to bed.

Before going to my room I went into Leroy and Ted's room. Between their two beds, on the wall, hung an embroidered. fancy piece of satin from the casket. "Mother" it said with red roses embroidered on it. Leroy was under the covers, his enormous eyes were all that showed. Ted was sitting up in bed.

"Hey, you guys, hey, I came on in to say goodnight. Your sign is pretty up there. Maybe tomorrow we can go down to the pond or something. Maybe the three of us can do something."

Ted looked at me like an old man. "Sure. They said I don't have to go to the Esso station to-morrow. I'll go down to the pond with you."

Leroy didn't say anything and started crying again. "I want my mother. They said God took her away. That's a crock of shit. God don't do evil things like that and if he does then I don't like him. If he's so good then let him bring my mother back." He screeched on like that and Carrie came hustling into the room. She sat down on the bed and held Leroy to soothe him. She gave him that line of crap about God and how we don't know what his plans are because we are only people and people are morons compared to God Almighty. Leroy stopped crying. Carrie rose and told me to "come on to bed and leave the boys alone." Leroy gave me a look, but I could only hold up my hands because she was dead set against me staying there. Ted slouched down on his bed, closed his eyes and looked one hundred years old. Carrie switched off the naked light bulb and there wasn't another sound.

I didn't stay in bed too long. I couldn't sleep thinking about Aunt Jenna there under the ground. What would happen if she'd open her eyes and see only dark and feel satin from the coffin? That'd scare her enough to kill her all over again. How do they know dead people don't open their eyes and see? They don't know nothing about being dead. Maybe they should have sat her in a chair along with other dead people. But I'd seen a very dead cow once and that made my thoughts worse. Was Aunt Jenna gonna swell up like that cow and turn black and smell and get full of maggots? I couldn't think about that, it tore my stomach right off its moorings. That's animals, same thing doesn't happen to people does it? That's gonna happen to me someday, too? No, not me. I ain't dying. I don't care what they say, I ain't dying. I'm not lying on my back under the ground in everlasting darkness. Not me. I'm not closing my eyes. If I close my eyes, I might not open them. Carrie was asleep so I crawled out of bed and crept down the hall covered with peeling green wallpaper with white gardenias on it. I was planning to hotfoot it out on the porch and watch the stars but I never made it because Ep and Carl were in the living room and Carl was holding Ep. He had both arms around him and every now and then he'd smooth down Ep's hair or put his cheek next to his head. Ep was crying just like Leroy. I couldn't make out what they were saying to each other. A couple times I could hear Carl telling Ep he had to hang on, that's all anybody can do is hang on. I was afraid they were going to get up and see me so I hurried back to my room. I'd never seen men hold each other. I thought the only things they were allowed to do was shake hands or fight. But if Carl was holding Ep maybe it wasn't against the rules. Since I wasn't sure, I thought I'd keep it to myself and never tell. I was glad they could touch each other. Maybe all men did that after everyone went to bed so no one would know the toughness was for show. Or maybe they only did it when someone died. I wasn't sure at all and it bothered me.

The next morning the sky was black with thunderclouds, and we had to spend the whole day in the house. The rain poured down and the leak by the kitchen table opened up again so Ted went out with shingles to patch it. After the storm the sky stayed dark but across the horizon was a brilliant rainbow. We all stared in silence for a long time, then went back inside. Ep stayed on the porch to look at the rainbow. Leroy bet me I couldn't find a pot of gold at the end, and I told him that was a stupid bet because the rainbow was enough.

Cheryl Spiegelglass lived on the other side of the
woods. Her daddy was a used car salesman and
they had more money than the rest of us in the
Hollow. Cheryl wore a dress, even when she didn't
have to. I hated her for that, plus she was always
sucking up to the adults. Carrie loved her and said
she looked exactly like Shirley Temple and why
didn't I look like that instead of roaming around
the fields in torn pants and dirty teeshirts. Cheryl
and I had been friends of a sort since first grade
so sometimes we played together. Carrie squirmed
like a dog with a new bone every time I'd go off to
the Spiegelglass's place, partly because she thought
I was moving into polite society and partly because
she hoped Cheryl would influence me for the
better. Leroy usually tagged along. Neither Leroy
nor I could stand it when Cheryl carted out her
dolls, so when she had doll days we steered clear.

One time Cheryl decided to play nurse and we put napkins on our heads. Leroy was the patient and we painted him with iodine so he'd look wounded. A nurse, I wasn't gonna be no nurse. If I was gonna be something I was gonna be the doctor and give orders. I tore off my napkin, and told Cheryl I was the new doctor in town. Her face corroded. "You can't be a doctor. Only boys can be doctors. Leroy's got to be the doctor."

"You're full of shit, Spiegelglass, Leroy's dumber than I am. I got to be the doctor because I'm the smart one and being a girl don't matter."

"You'll see. You think you can do what boys do but you're going to be a nurse, no two ways about it. It doesn't matter about brains, brains don't count. What counts is whether you're a boy or a girl."

I hauled off and belted her one. Shirley Temple Spiegelglass wasn't gonna tell me I couldn't be a doctor, nor nobody else. Course I didn't want to be a doctor. I was going to be president only I kept it a secret. But if I wanted to be a doctor I'd go be one and ain't nobody gonna tell me otherwise. So I got in trouble, of course. Cheryl went snotty-nosed into her mother and showed her the split lip I just gave her. Ethel Spiegelglass, mother hen, came flying out of that house, with the real aluminum awnings on it, and grabbed me by the teeshirt and gave me a piece of her mind, which was very uncomplimentary to me. She told me I couldn't see Cheryl for a week. That was fine with me. I didn't want to see nobody who'd tell me I couldn't be a doctor. Leroy and I started home.

"You really gonna be a doctor, Molly?"

"No, I ain't. I'm gonna be something lots better

than a doctor. If you're a doctor you have to look at scabs and blood, besides only people in one place know your name. I got to be something that everybody knows my name. I'm going to be great."

"Great what?"

"That's a secret."

"Tell, come on, you can tell me, I'm your best friend."

"No, but I'll tell you when you're old enough to vote."

"When's that?"

"When you're twenty-one."

"That's ten years from now. I might be dead. I'll be an old man. Tell me now."

"No. Forget it. Anyway, whatever I am, I'll make sure you get some of the goodies so let me do it my own way."

Leroy settled for that, but with rancor.

We got home and Carrie was hopping mad. Somehow, between my splitting Cheryl's lip and us walking home, she gathered the news. "You big-mouthed brat. Can't play nice, can you? Can't act like a lady, no way. You're a heathen, that's what you are. You going up there and hitting that sweet child. How could you do such a thing? How am I gonna show my face around here? And you doing such a thing so soon after Jenna's passed away. You got no sense of respect. God knows, I've tried to bring you up right. You're not my child. You're wild, some wild animal. Your father must have been an ape or something."

Leroy's mouth fell open. He didn't know about me yet. Damn, I could have killed Carrie for shooting her big mouth off right then. Why'd she have to lay me out in front of fat Leroy? She's the one with no respect.

She ran on and she got me for this offense and that offense as well as one hundred trespasses. She's gonna make a lady out of me that summer, a crash program. She was going to keep me in the house to teach me to act right, cook, clean, and sew and that scared me.

"I can learn them things at night, you don't have to keep me in the house during the day."

"You're staying in this house with me, Miss Molly. No more going out with the roughhouse Hollow gang. That's one of the things wrong with you that I can fix. Your blood's another matter."

Leroy sat down quietly at the table and played with the diagonal pattern on the tablecloth. He wasn't liking this no more than I was. "If Molly stays in then I stay in."

Leroy, I love you.

"You ain't staying in here, Leroy Denman. You're a boy and you go out and play like boys are supposed to do. It's not right for you to learn those things."

"I don't care. I'm going where Molly goes. She's my best friend and my cousin and we got to stick together."

Carrie tried to reason with Leroy but he wouldn't budge until she started telling him what would happen to him if he picked up women's ways. Now old Leroy was shaking. Everybody would point at him and laugh. Nobody would play with him if he stayed in with me and soon they'd take him to the hospital and cut his thing off. Leroy sold out.

"Okay, Aunt Carrie, I won't stay in the house."
He looked at me with utter defeat and guilt.

Leroy you ain't no friend of mine.

Carrie went down into the root cellar to get jars
and rubber rings. Canning was going to be my
first lesson. Before she hit the last step I leaped
at the door, shut it, and locked it. She didn't
notice it until she was ready to come up. Then she
called out, "Molly, Leroy, door's shut, let me out."

Leroy was scared shitless. "Molly, let her out or
they'll beat both of us good. Ep will get out the
strap. You let her out."

"You take one step toward that door Leroy
Denman and I'll slit your throat." I picked up the
carving knife to make my words true. Leroy was
between the devil and the deep blue sea.

"Molly, let me outa this root cellar!"

"I ain't lettin' you outa that root cellar until you
promise to let me go free. Till you promise I don't
have to stay in this house and learn to sew."

"I'll promise no such thing."

"Then you staying in that root cellar until Jesus
comes back." I walked out the door and slammed
it so she could hear, dragging Leroy with me every
step of the way. No one was home. Florence was
down at West York Market. Ted was at the Esso
station, and Carl and Ep were at work. No one
could hear her pounding on that door and screaming her lungs out except Leroy and me. Her
screams just scalded Leroy. "She's dying in there.
You got to let her out. She'll go blind in the dark.
Molly, please let her out."

"She ain't dying in there, she ain't going blind
and I ain't lettin' her out."

"What'd she mean about you not being her child? About you being an animal?"

"She don't know what she's talking about. Talking through her hat. Don't pay no attention to her."

"Well, you don't look like her nor Carl neither. You don't look like any of us. Maybe you ain't hers. You're the only one in the Hollow with black hair and brown eyes. Hey, maybe she found you in the bull rushes like Moses."

"Shut up, Leroy." He was on the track. He was bound to find out sooner or later, since Carrie let the cat outa the bag so I guessed I'd have to tell him. "It's true what she says. I ain't hers. I don't belong to nobody. I got no true mother nor father and I ain't your real cousin. And this ain't my home. But it don't matter. It matters to her when she gets mad at me. She says I'm a bastard then. But it don't matter to me. But we're still cousins in our own way. Blood's just something old people talk about to make you feel bad. Hey Leroy, you don't care none, do you?"

Leroy was buckling under the weight of the news. "If we ain't true cousins then what are we? We got to be something."

"We're friends, though we might as well be cousins cause we're together all the time."

"What does it mean, bastard? What's the difference between you and me if you ain't Carrie and Carl's?"

"It means that your mother, Jenna, was married to Ep when she had you and my mother, whoever she is, wasn't married to my dad, whoever he is. That's exactly what it means."

35

"Well hell, Molly, what's being married?"

"It's a piece of paper, that's all I can figure. Some people don't even have to stand in front of a preacher, so it ain't religion. You can go on down to the courthouse and sign up like Uncle Ep signed up for the Marine Corps. Then you hear words said over you and you both sign this piece of paper and you're married."

"Could we get married?"

"Sure, but we got to be old, fifteen or sixteen, at least."

"That's only four more years, Molly. Let's get married."

"Leroy, we don't need to get married. We're together all the time. It's silly to get married. Besides I'm never gettin' married."

"Everybody gets married. It's something you have to do, like dying."

"I ain't doin' it."

"I don't know, Molly, you're headin' for a hard life. You say you're gonna be a doctor or something great. Then you say you ain't gettin' married. You have to do some of the things everybody does or people don't like you."

"I don't care whether they like me or not. Everybody's stupid, that's what I think. I care if I like me, that's what I truly care about."

"Now that's the damndest dumb thing I ever heard. Everybody likes themself. Fact, Florence says you got to learn not to like yourself so much and like other people."

"Since when have you started listening to Florence? I can't like anybody if I don't like myself. Period."

"Molly, you are flat out crazy. Everybody likes themself, I am telling you."

"Oh yeah, smartass? Did you like yourself when you told Carrie you'd go out and play and leave me trapped inside with a sewing basket?"

Leroy's face flashed shame. Bull's eye. He switched the subject to save himself having to think on that one any more. "If you're not gonna get married then I won't either. Why do people get married anyway?"

"So's they can fuck."

"What?" Leroy's voice went into a high-pitched trail.

"Fuck."

"Molly Bolt, that is a dirty word."

"Dirty or not, that's what they do."

"Do you know what it means?"

"Not exactly but it has something to do with taking all your clothes off and messing around. Remember how upset Florence got when those two dogs were stuck together? That's what it is, I think. I don't know why anyone would want to do it, because those dogs didn't look very happy about it. I know that's what it is, besides I seen dirty books Ted hides under his mattress and you should see them. It'd make you sick for sure."

"Dirty books?"

"Yeah, Ted's been reading them ever since his voice started cracking. You ask me, I think his mind is cracking right along with it, myself."

"How'd you find out he was reading them?"

"Spied on him. After you go to sleep he turns the light back on so I knew he was up to something and I snuck out for a peek. There he was

37

reading. Now the only books in this house are the Bible and our school books. I know he ain't reading none of them."

"You are truly smart, Molly," Leroy said with admiration.

"Yeah, I know."

Carrie's screams and poundings had died down by this time. "Let's go back and see if she is ready to make a deal."

A soft whimper came from behind the cellar door when I knocked on it. "Mom, you ready to come out now? You ready to make that deal?"

"I'm ready, just let me outa this dark hole. It's full of bugs."

I unbolted the door and opened it. Carrie was sitting on the root cellar steps like a little girl, holding her arms and crunched over. She looked up at me with pure hate and flew out of the cellar like a jack-in-the-box. She grabbed me by the hair before I could dodge and started hitting me in the face, stomach, and when I doubled over like a porcupine, she hit me on the back with both fists at once. I could feel my eye start to close up already. I was so busy trying to get away from her that I didn't hear what she was calling me. Leroy fled the house in total terror. He didn't once try to gang up on her. If he'd blasted her with a couple good kicks, I might have gotten away. But Leroy never was tactical, plus he had a streak of the coward in him.

That night I was sent to bed without supper. I didn't care because I couldn't eat my supper anyway. My mouth was all swelled up ugly, and it hurt to talk. The whole crew got Carrie's version of my sins and I couldn't open my mouth in self-defense. I guess she thought she'd shame me in front of all of them, but I stared at her with real pride as I marched into the bedroom. She wasn't going to beat me down, no how. Let'em all get mad at me, I wasn't giving her a goddamned inch, not one. I crawled in bed but I was so sore I couldn't sleep and late that night I heard Carrie and Carl get in a blowout. Only time I ever heard Carl raise his voice, and I bet the rest of the house heard him too. "Carrie, the child's high-spirited and she's smart, you got to remember that. That kid's quicker than all of us put together. She started reading all by herself when she was three with no help from any of us. You got to treat her with some respect for her brains. She's a good girl, just full of life and the devil, that's all."

"I don't give a goddamn how brainy she is, she don't act natural. It ain't right for a girl to be running all around with the boys at all hours. She climbs trees, takes cars apart, and worse, she tells them what to do and they listen to her. She don't want to learn none of the things she has to know to get a husband. Smart as she is, a woman can't get on in this world without a husband. We can't be sending no girl to school as it is. It's the boys we got to worry about. Them's the ones will be earning livings. You make too much of her head."

"Molly is going to college."

"Big talk."

"My daughter is going to college."

"Your daughter, your daughter. That's a laugh. That's the first time I heard you say that. She's

Ruby Drollinger's bastard that's who she is. Where do you get off with this daughter crap?"

"She's mine as much as if I'd been her real father and I watch out for her."

"Real father. What right have you got to talk about being a real father? If you'd been a real father I'd have my own daughter and she wouldn't be like that wild hellcat you stick up for. She'd be a real little lady like Cheryl Spiegelglass. Your daughter, you make me sick."

"Honey, you're all upset. You don't know how you're sounding. Molly is yours, just as if she was your own. A child's got to have parents and you're her mother."

"I am not her mother. I am not her mother," Carrie shrieked. "She didn't come from my body. Florence had babies come from her body, and she tells me it's not the same. She knows. She told me I'll never know what it's like to be a real mother. What do you know? Men don't know about these things. Men don't know anything."

"Mother, father, what's the difference, Cat? It's how you feel about the child, it's got nothing to do with your body. Molly is my daughter, and if it's the last thing I do, I'm going to see that girl gets a chance in this world neither one of us had. You want her to spend her life like us, sitting back here in the sticks, can't even make enough money for a new dress or dinner in a restaurant? You want her to live a life like you—dishes, cooking, and never going out except maybe to a movie once a month if we can afford it? The child's got brightness in her, Cat, so let her be! She'll go to big cities and be somebody. I can see it in her.

She's got dreams and ambition and she's smart as a whip. Nobody can pull one over on that kid. Be proud for her. You got a daughter to be proud of."

"You turn my guts. She'll be somebody. That's all I need, Molly traipsing off to a big city like Philadelphia and thinking she's better than the rest of us. She's got high ways now. You make her worse. She'll go off to college and a big city and forget you ever lived. That's the thanks you'll get. She don't care for nobody but her own self, that kid. She's a savage animal, locked me in the cellar. You don't live here with her every day and see her like I do. She's wild I tell you. And how far's she gonna get with all her brains considering her background? We ain't people that can do her good in fancy places. She'll be ashamed of us. And she's a bastard to boot. You got pipe dreams for your daughter." She hit on daughter with such bile it made me shudder.

"Cat, my mind is made up. Molly is having her chance whether you like it or not. She's getting an education. Now you learn to live with it, and you're not to lock her in this house with you. Let her run all over the whole goddamn county and let her knock shit out of Cheryl Spiegelglass. I never liked that kid anyway."

"I have one think to say to you, Carl Bolt. We've never had a fight between us until that child came under our roof. And we never would have a fight like this if you could have given me a baby, but you had syphilis, that's what you had. You ain't fit to be nobody's father. If I could have had my own all this would be different. This is all your doing and I'll never forget it."

"My mind's made up." His voice was soft with hurt feelings.

"We'll just see about that," Carrie hedged. She had to get the last word in, whether anyone listened or not.

Leota B. Bisland sat next to me that year in sixth grade, and Leroy sat behind. Leota was the most beautiful girl I had ever seen. She was tall and slender with creamy skin and deep, green eyes. She was quiet and shy so I spent most of sixth grade concentrating on making Leota laugh. Miss Potter wasn't too pleased with my performance in the first row but she was a sweet old soul and only made me stand in the hall once. That didn't work out, because I kept returning to the doorway to dance when Miss Potter's head was turned. I also made the finger at Leroy. Right when I was in the middle of shooting the bird, Miss Potter turns from the blackboard. "Molly, since you enjoy performing so much I'm going to make you the star of the Christmas play this year." Leroy asked whether the play was going to be *The Creature from the Black Lagoon*. Naturally everybody screamed. Miss Potter said no, it was a play about the nativity of Jesus and I was to be Virgin Mary.

Cheryl Spiegelglass got so mad she jumped up and said, "But Miss Potter, the Virgin Mary was the mother of little Lord Jesus and she was the most perfect woman on earth. Virgin Mary has to be played by a good girl and Molly isn't good. Yesterday she stuck a wad of bubble gum in Audrey's hair." Cheryl was bucking to be Virgin Mary, that was clear. Miss Potter said that we had to consider dramatic talent not just whether a person was good or not. Besides, maybe if I played the Virgin Mary some of her goodness would rub off.

Leota was a lady of Bethlehem so she was in the play too. And Cheryl was Joseph. Miss Potter said this would be a great challenge to Cheryl. She was also in charge of costumes, probably because her father would donate them. Anyway she got her name in the program twice in big letters.

Leroy was a Wise Man, and he wore a long beard with Little Lulu curls on it. We all had to stay after school every day to remember our lines and rehearse. Miss Potter was right, I was so busy trying to get everything perfect that I didn't have time to get into trouble or think about anything else except Leota. I began to wonder if girls could marry girls, because I was sure I wanted to marry Leota and look in her green eyes forever. But I would only marry her if I didn't have to do the housework. I was certain of that. But if Leota really didn't want to do it either, I guessed I'd do it. I'd do anything for Leota.

Leroy began to get mad that I was paying so

much attention to a mere village inhabitant and he was a Wise Man. He forgot it as soon as I gave him my penknife with the naked lady on it that I clipped from Earl Stambach.

The Christmas pageant was an enormous production. All the mothers came, and it was so important that they even took off work. Cheryl's father was sitting right in the front row in the seat of honor. Carrie and Florence showed up to marvel at me being Virgin Mary and at Leroy in robes. Leroy and I were so excited we could barely stand it, and we got to wear makeup, rouge and red lipstick. Getting painted was so much fun that Leroy confessed he liked it too, although boys aren't supposed to, of course. I told him not to worry about it, because he had a beard and if you had a beard, it must be all right to wear lipstick if you wanted to because everyone will know you're a man. He thought that sounded reasonable and we made a pact to run away as soon as we were old enough and go be famous actors. Then we could wear pretty clothes all the time, never pick potato bugs, and wear lipstick whenever we felt like it. We vowed to be so wonderful in this show that our fame would spread to the people who run theaters.

Cheryl overheard our plans and sneered, "You can do all you please, but everyone is going to look at me because I have the most beautiful blue cloak in the whole show."

"Nobody's gonna know it's you because you're playing Joseph and that'll throw them off. Ha," Leroy gloated.

"That's just why they'll all notice me, because I'll have to be specially skilled to be a good Joseph.

45

Anyway, who is going to notice Virgin Mary, all she does is sit by the crib and rock Baby Jesus. She doesn't say much. Any dumb person can be Virgin Mary, all you have to do is put a halo over her head. It takes real talent to be Joseph, especially when you're a girl."

The conversation didn't get finished because Miss Potter bustled backstage. "Hush, children, curtain's almost ready to go up. Molly, Cheryl, get in your places."

When the curtain was raised there was a rustle of anticipation in the maternal audience. Megaphone Mouth said above all the whispers, "Isn't she dear up there?"

And dear I was. I looked at Baby Jesus with the tenderest looks I could manufacture and all the while my antagonist, Cheryl, had her hand on my shoulder digging me with her fingernails and a staff in her right hand. A record went on the phonograph and "Noel" began to play. The Wise Men came in most solemnly. Leroy carried a big gold box and presented it to me. I said, "Thank you, O King, for you have traveled far." And Cheryl, that rat, says, "And traveled far," as loud as she could. She wasn't supposed to say that. She started saying whatever came in her head that sounded religious. Leroy was choking in his beard and I was rocking the cradle so hard that the Jesus doll fell on the floor. So I decided two can play this game. I leaned over the doll and said in my most gentle voice, "O, dearest babe, I hope you have not hurt yourself. Come let Mother put you back to bed." Well, Leroy was near to dying of perplexity and he started to say something too, but Cheryl cut him off with, "Don't worry, Mary, babies fall out of the cradle all the time." That wasn't enough for greedy-guts, she then goes on about how she was a carpenter in a foreign land and how we had to travel many miles just so I could have my baby. She rattled on and on. All that time she spent in Sunday School was paying off because she had one story after another. I couldn't stand it any longer so I blurted out in the middle of her tale about the tax collectors, "Joseph, you shut up or you'll wake the baby." Miss Potter was aghast in the wings, and the shepherds didn't know what to do because they were back there waiting to come on. As soon as I told Joseph to shut up, Miss Potter pushed the shepherds on the stage. "We saw a star from afar," Robert Prather warbled, "and we came to worship the newborn Prince." Just then Barry Aldridge, another shepherd, peed right there on the stage he was so scared. Joseph saw her chance and said in an imperious voice, "You can't pee in front of little Lord Jesus, go back to the hills." That made me mad. "He can pee where he wants to, this is a stable, ain't it?" Joseph stretched to her full height, and began to push Barry off the stage with her staff. I jumped out of my chair, and wrenched the staff out of her hand. She grabbed it back. "Go sit down, you're supposed to watch out for the baby. What kind of mother are you?"

"I ain't sittin' nowhere until you button your fat lip and do this right."

We struggled and pushed each other, until I caught her off balance and she tripped on her long cloak. As she started to fall, I gave her a shove and she flew off the stage into the audience. Miss Potter zoomed out on the stage, took my hand and said in a calm voice, "Now ladies and gentlemen, let's sing songs appropriate to the season." Miss Martin at the piano struck up "O Come All Ye Faithful."

Cheryl was down there among the folding chairs bawling her eyes out. Miss Potter pulled me off stage, where I had started to sing. I knew I was in for it.

"Now, Molly, Cheryl did wrong to talk out of turn, but you shouldn't have shoved her off the stage." Then she let me go, not even a little slap. Leroy was as surprised as I was. "It's a good thing she ain't mad but wait until Aunt Carrie and Florence get a hold of you."

True enough, Carrie nearly lost her liver with rage and I had to stay in the house for a solid week and all that time I had to do the chores: dishes, ironing, wash, even cooking. That made me give up the idea of marrying Leota B. Bisland if she wouldn't do the chores or at least half of them. I had to figure out a way to find out what Leota would agree to.

That week I thought of how to ask Leota to marry me. I'd die in front of her and ask her in my last breath. If she said yes, I'd miraculously recover. I'd send her a note on colored paper with a white dove. I'd ride over to her house on Barry Aldridge's horse, sing her a song like in the movies, then she'd get on the back of the horse and we'd ride off into the sunset. None of them seemed right so I decided to come straight out and ask.

Next Monday after school Leroy, Leota, and I were walking home. I gave Leroy a dime and told him to go on ahead to Mrs. Hershener's for an ice cream. He offered no resistance as his stomach always came first.

"Leota, you thought about getting married?"

"Yeah, I'll get married and have six children and wear an apron like my mother, only my husband will be handsome."

"Who you gonna marry?"

"I don't know yet."

"Why don't you marry me? I'm not handsome, but I'm pretty."

"Girls can't get married."

"Says who?"

"It's a rule."

"It's a dumb rule. Anyway, you like me better than anybody, don't you? I like you better than anybody."

"I like you best, but I still think girls can't get married."

"Look, if we want to get married, we can get married. It don't matter what anybody says. Besides Leroy and I are running away to be famous actors. We'll have lots of money and clothes and we can do what we want. Nobody dares tell you what to do if you're famous. Now ain't that a lot better than sitting around here with an apron on?"

"Yes."

"Good. Then let's kiss like in the movies and we'll be engaged."

We threw our arms around each other and kissed. My stomach felt funny.

"Does your stomach feel strange?"

"Kinda."

"Let's do it again."

We kissed again and my stomach felt worse.

After that, Leota and I went off by ourselves each day after school. Somehow we knew enough not to go around kissing in front of everyone, so we went into the woods and kissed until it was time to go home. Leroy was beside himself, because I didn't walk home with him anymore. One day he trailed us into the woods and burst in on us like a triumphant police sergeant.

"Kissing. You two come out here kissing. I'm gonna tell everyone in the whole world."

"Well now, Leroy Denman, what you want to tell for? Maybe you ought to try it before you shoot your big mouth off. You might want to come here after school too."

Temptation shone in Leroy's eyes, he never wanted to miss anything, but he hedged. "I don't want to go kissing girls."

"Kiss the cows then, Leroy. There's nothin' else to kiss. It feels good. You're sure missing some fun."

He began to weaken. "Do I have to close my eyes if I kiss you?"

"Yes. You can't kiss and keep your eyes open, they'll cross forever."

"I don't want to close my eyes."

"All right then, stupid, keep your eyes open. What do I care if you got cross-eyes. It's not my problem if you don't want to do it right."

"Who do I kiss first?"

"Whoever you want."

"I'll kiss you first, since I know you better." Leroy puckered up and gave me a kiss like Florence gives at night.

"Leroy, that ain't right. You got your mouth all screwed up. Don't squinch it together like that."

50

Leota was laughing, and she reached out to Leroy with a long arm, drew him to her and gave him a fat kiss. Leroy began to get the idea.

"Watch us," Leota advised. We finished a kiss, then I gave Leroy another one. He was getting a little better at it, although he was still stiff.

"How's your stomach feel."

"Hungry, why?"

"Don't your stomach feel funny at all?" Leota asked.

"No."

"Maybe it's different for boys," she said.

After that the three of us went off after school. It was okay having Leroy around but he never did get to be an accomplished kisser. There were times when I felt kissing Leota wasn't enough, but I wasn't sure what the next step would be. So until I knew, I settled for kissing. I knew about fucking and getting stuck together like dogs and I didn't want to get stuck like that. It was very confusing. Leota was full of ideas. Once she laid down on top of me to give me a kiss and I knew that was a step in the right direction, until Leroy piled on and my lungs near caved in. I thought maybe we'd do it again when Leroy wasn't around.

Leroy convinced me not to tell anyone that we were kissing and all going to be famous. He figured it was another one of those rules and the grownups would keep us from running away to act. And the grownups did keep us three from running away together, but not because we were kissing in the woods.

One bitter night in February with the oven on and the gas heaters going, all the adults asked us into the kitchen. They told us we were moving to

Florida as soon as school was over. There'd be warm weather all year round, and you could pick oranges right off the trees. I didn't believe it, of course. It can't be warm all year round. Another trick, but I didn't say anything. Carrie assured us we'd like it because we could swim in the ocean, and jobs were easier to find so there'd be something for everybody. Then they put us all to bed. Going to Florida wasn't so bad. They didn't have to tell lies to get me to go. I just didn't want to leave Leota, that's all.

The next day I told Leota the news and she didn't like it any more than I did, but there seemed to be nothing we could do about it. We promised to write each other and to keep going out into the woods until the very last day.

Spring came late that year and the roads were muddy. Carrie and Florence had already gone through the house, throwing things out, packing things we didn't need for everyday use. By May everything was ready to go save for a few kitchen utensils, the clothes we wore, and a few pieces of furniture in the living room. Every day I felt a little worse about it. Kissing in the woods made it worse. Even Leroy started to feel the pinch, and he didn't care about Leota or kissing quite the way I did. It seemed like if I was going to leave I ought to leave knowing more than kissing. Leota wasn't far from the same conclusion. One week before school ended she asked me to spend the night with her. She had a bedroom all to herself so we wouldn't have to share it with her little sister, and her mother said I could stay over. This was one time things worked in my favor. There was no question that Leroy could be asked to spend the night. If Carrie wouldn't let me sleep in Leroy's room, it was a sure bet that nobody was going to let Leroy spend the night at Leota's. Leroy didn't care much anyway. Sleep was sleep to Leroy.

I put my toothbrush, pajamas and comb in a paper bag and walked down the road to the Bislands. You could see their house from far away because they had a t.v. aerial on it. We stayed up and watched the Milton Berle show. He kept getting pies in the face and everyone thought that was so funny. I didn't think it was so funny. They should have eaten the pies instead of throwing them at each other. If they were mad why didn't they just knock the crap out of each other? It made no sense to me but it was fun to watch. I didn't care if Milton Berle didn't know better.

After the show, we got into bed and pulled up the sheets. Leota's mother closed the door and shut off the lights because they were still watching t.v. That was fine with us. Soon as the door was shut we started kissing. We must have kissed for hours but I couldn't really tell because I didn't think about anything except kissing. We did hear her parents turn off the t.v. and go to bed. Then Leota decided we'd try lying on top of one another. We did that but it made my stomach feel terrible.

"Molly, let's take our pajamas off and do that."

"Okay, but we got to remember to put them back on before morning." It was much better without the pajamas. I could feel her cool skin all over my body. That really was a lot better. Leota started kissing me with her mouth open. Now my stomach was going to fall out on the floor. Great, I am found dead in the Bisland home with my stomach hanging outa my mouth. "Leota, that makes my stomach hurt a lot more but it's kinda good too."

"Mine too."

We kept on. If we were going to die from stomach trouble we were resolved to die together. She began to touch me all over and I knew I was really going to die. Leota was bold. She wasn't afraid to touch anything and where her knowledge came from was a secret but she knew what she was after. And I soon found out.

The next morning we went to school like any two sixth-grade girls. I fell asleep during fractions. Leroy gave me a poke and snickered. Leota looked at me with those dreamy eyes and I hurt all over again. We couldn't move to Florida, we just couldn't.

But we did. Leota came down on the day we packed up the old Dodge truck and the 1940 Packard. She and I hung around while Carrie put the last things away then called me to the car. I threw my arms around her neck and kissed her then ran to the car. We wrote a few times after that, then the letters drifted off. I didn't see Leota again until 1968.

Our raggedy caravan kept to the coast as we moved slowly through the flatlands of the South. Carl and Ep detoured to take us kids to Richmond and there we saw a stuffed seal that had come down to swim around Richmond in the 1800s. There was a stuffed Indian too, but he made me sick. Leroy, Ted, and I liked the Civil War uniforms best. The Confederate ones were the prettiest because they had gold braid all down on the cuffs of the sleeves. Leroy confessed if he didn't become a famous actor, he'd become a soldier so he could wear gold braid on his sleeves. I said that was okay but then he couldn't wear lipstick and he'd have to follow orders.

The journey dragged on and we nearly went crazy cooped up in the car. Carrie invented a license plate game that helped. First one to get one hundred points wins. The plates of the state you were going through counted one point. Every state in the South aside from that state was two points. Northern states were five points and Midwestern ones were ten. Western states were twenty points and California plates were thirty. I knew we'd never see California plates because only movie stars lived out there, and why'd they want to be driving around these washed-out lands?

Once in Athens, Georgia, we pulled over to eat and go to the bathroom. Leroy, Ted, and I popped out of the car and zoomed into the dinky restaurant that smelled of years of grease. I sped past the door the boys used and into the next one. Carrie seized my arm as I was coming out.

"You got no sense, girl. You do that again and I'm gonna whale you good, you hear me? That's the colored room and you stay out." I wasn't about to argue with her in front of strangers, but when we got back in the car I asked Carl what all that meant. Carrie turned to him, "See, she won't listen to me. You make her listen."

"Down South things are a little different than up in York. Here the whites and the coloreds don't mix and you're not to mess with those people, although you are to be mannerly should you ever have to talk to one. Your mother was trying to save you from getting in trouble someday."

"Daddy, that's no different than up home in York. They just don't put 'Colored' over the bathroom doors, that's all."

"You little smartmouth, you shut your trap," Carrie warned.

"No, I ain't shutting my mouth. It's no different except for the signs. I ain't gonna sit here and pretend it's different when it ain't." Leroy tugged my sleeve fearing a fight. I gave him a jab. "Daddy, why should I shut up?"

"You got a point there, kid, but around here people get more riled up about coloreds than they do in the North. Other than that, you're right. I can't see it's no different neither." Carrie said we were both teched and looked glumly out the window.

"Since I don't know who my real folks are maybe they're colored. Maybe it's all right for me to go in those bathrooms."

"My God!" Carrie exploded, "if you ain't enough trouble now you want to go be a nigger."

Carl laughed and the sun caught on his gold tooth and reflected back on the window. "It'd show, Molly. Who knows what you are, you're a mongrel, that's all."

"She's darker than the rest of us, Uncle Carl." Leroy piped up.

"She's got brown eyes, none of us got brown eyes."

"Lots of people have brown eyes and are olive complected; Italians and Spaniards are like that."

"Hey Molly, maybe you're a spic," Leroy offered.

"I don't care what the hell I am. And I ain't staying away from people because they look different."

Carrie whirled around in a full fury and spat. "If I ever see you mixing with the wrong kind, I'm gonna wring your neck, brat. You try it and see how far you get."

"Cat, children don't understand these things.

59

No reason to get so upset. Your mother's trying to save you trouble, Molly. Let it lie."

When we hit Florida, we were all excited but that didn't last long. We drove and drove and it was still Florida. Florence said we were going down the east coast to the southern tip because that's where all the jobs and money were. Finally we pulled up in Ft. Lauderdale. Carl said Miami was full of Jews, so he'd try this place first. I couldn't believe there'd be a whole city where people walked around with their hands in their pants, but I didn't ask. Ft. Lauderdale was laced with canals and palm trees, and everyone liked it a lot. Within a week Carl had found a job in a butcher shop in the northeast of the city. Ep got one the week after that putting jalousie windows in houses, but the company wanted him to move up to West Palm Beach. He said he would, so Leroy, Ted and Ep moved up to Loxahachee and lived in a trailer. It looked like a fat silver larva squatted on four acres of scrub. We didn't get a trailer but a house next to the Florida East Coast Railway and behind an electrical power plant that hummed constantly. The only time you couldn't hear the hum was when the train came through. Every Sunday we went up to Loxahachee or Leroy, Ted, and Ep came down to see us. Leroy had a .22 rifle and thought he was hot shit. Ted was working after school in another gas station and I was mostly hanging around Holiday Park because there was nothing else to do and Carrie wouldn't let me have a .22.

That September I went to Naval Air Junior High School, a makeshift school in Navy barracks leftover from World War II. The teachers were leftover too, and I was bored out of my mind. I kept to myself to see who was who in that place before I made any friends. There were a fair amount of rich kids at Naval Air. You could tell them by their clothes and the way they talked. I knew enough from English lessons by this time to know they had good grammar. They held themselves away from the red-neck kids. I didn't mix with anybody. I knew I wasn't rich but then I wasn't walking around with little plastic clothespins on my collar like all the red-neck girls either. The boys were much worse than the girls. They had long greasy hair and wore denim jackets with bloody eyeballs drawn on them. Hot as hell, they'd wear those denim jackets and black motorcycle boots and they were dirty mouthed to go along with it.

Back in the Hollow we were all the same. Maybe Cheryl Spiegelglass had a little more, but the gap didn't seem so wide. Here it was a distinct line drawn between two camps and I was certain I didn't want to be on the side with the greasy boys that leered at me and talked filthy. But I had no money. It took me all of seventh grade to figure out how I would take care of myself in this new situation, but I did figure it out.

For one thing I made good grades and they counted for a lot. You couldn't go to college without good grades. Even in junior high school, the rich kids talked about college. If I made those grades, I'd get a scholarship, then I'd go too. I also had to stop talking the way we talked at home. I could think bad grammar all I wanted, but I learned rapidly not to speak it. Then there was the problem of clothes. I couldn't afford all those clothes. The next fall, when Carrie took me to a Lerner Shop for my wardrobe, I told her I didn't want two-dollar blouses from Lerner's. She didn't get mad like I expected. In fact, she seemed pleased that I was taking an interest in my appearance. It gave her hope for my femininity. She agreed that I could buy a few good things from a better store. Kids at school may have noticed that I wore the same things a lot, but at least they were good things. And I knew I couldn't make my way by throwing parties. What would we all do, dance to the power plant hum? Anyway, I wasn't up for bringing those snots home. I decided to become the funniest person in the whole school. If someone makes you laugh you have to like her. I even made my teachers laugh. It worked.

It was about this time during the last of eighth grade that Leroy and I began to understand we weren't going to run away together and become famous actors. One Sunday when the ixora were in full bloom and everything was bright red we went up to Loxahachee. Leroy and I were down by the canal at Old Powerline Road, fishing. Leroy wasn't a tub anymore. He had grown his hair into a d.a. that curled over his denim jacket with the bloody eyeballs on it.

"Hey, is it true you're flunking out this year?"

"Yeah, the old man is ready to take the strap to me but I don't give a damn. School's stupid. There's nothing they can teach me. I want to go make money and buy me a Bonneville Triumph like Craig's."

"Me too, and I'd paint mine candy apple red."

"You can't have one. Girls can't have motorcycles."

"Fuck you, Leroy. I'll buy an army tank if I want to and run over anyone who tells me I can't have it."

Leroy cocked his slicked head and looked at me. "You know, I think you're a queer."

"So what if I am, except I'm not real sure what you mean by that."

"I mean you ain't natural, that's what I mean. It's time you started worrying about your hair and doing those things that girls are supposed to do."

"Since when are you telling me what to do, lardass? I can still lay you out flat." Leroy backed off a few paces, because he knew it was true and he wasn't up for no fight especially since we were near a bed of sandspurs. "How come you're all of a sudden so interested in my being a lady?"

"I dunno. I like you the way you are, but then I get confused. If you're doing what you please, out there riding around on motorcycles, then what am I supposed to do? I mean how do I know how to act if you act the same way?"

"What goddamn difference does it make to you what I do? You do what you want and I do what I want."

"Maybe I don't know what I want," his voice wavered. "Besides, I'm a chicken and you're not. You really would go around on a candy apple red Triumph and give people the finger when they stared at you. I don't want people down on me." Leroy started to cry. I pulled him close to me, and we sat on the bank of the canal that was stinking in the noon sun.

"Hey, what is it? You gotta be crying over more than me fixing my hair and riding a bike. Tell me. You know I'll never tell."

"I'm all mixed up. First, there's the gang at school. They're all tough and if I don't act tough, they'll whip my ass and laugh me right outa the school. I got to smoke and swear and take cars apart. I like taking cars apart, but I don't care about the smoking and the swearing, you know? But you gotta do it. You don't do it and they say you're queer."

"You mean queer for real—sucking-cock queer?"

"Yeah, and there's this one poor bastard, oh, sorry, there's this one poor guy, Joel Centers. Joel's skinny and tall and he likes school. He does his lessons everyday and he likes English class best of all. English. You should see what they do to him. Nobody's doing that to me."

"Who cares what those dumb jocks think? Anyway, you can play along with them, and as soon as we both get out of high school we can hotfoot it up to a big city. We can do what we want then. And that's only four years away."

"Might as well be a hundred. I got to worry about right now and at the rate I'm going, I'm not getting outa high school in four years. I'm sure to flunk a few more times."

"So we wait until I get out, then we leave. It's not so impossible."

"Yes it is. You're different than I am. You make good grades and know how to act with different kinds of people who aren't like us. I can't do those things."

"You can learn. You're not deaf, dumb, and blind."

"Sure, then they'll call me a queer for sure."

"Leroy, you are harping very heavy on this queer thing. First you tell me I'm a queer, and now you are so worried everybody's gonna think you're one. You look like an ordinary person. What are you worried about?"

"You swear never to tell. You promise me?"

"Yes."

"Well, a couple of weeks ago I was down at Jack's Gulf station where Ted's working, you know? So there's this old guy, Craig, hangs around there. He's maybe 25 or something like that and he lifts weights, you should see his muscles. And he's got the biggest, hottest Triumph in all Palm Beach County. He's all the time taking me for rides. He don't look like no queer to me. Not with all those muscles and that deep voice. We're getting to be friends, him and me. The guys at school really get jealous when they see me on that bike, you know. Nearly kills them. So one night we got out drinking, I didn't get drunk, just feelin good. We were out near to Belle Blade, out in the scrubs and well, Craig puts his hand on my crotch. I was scared shitless but it felt good. He gives me this blow job and it felt great, really great. So now I'm scared. Really scared. Maybe I'm a queer. Damn, the old man finds out, Ted, they'll kill me for sure."

"You tell anybody besides me?"

"No, you think I'm crazy? You're the only one in the world I can tell because I think maybe you're queer too. I remember all of us kissing on old Leota B. Bisland."

"You seen Craig again?"

"I stayed away from the station for a couple of days after that. I couldn't face him. Then he came tearing down the road to the trailer after I got home from school, and nobody's home so we talked and he tells me not to worry. He's not telling anyone, because they'll throw him in jail for corrupting a minor. Then he tells me he loves me and tried to kiss me. I may be queer but I ain't kissing no man. But I let him suck me off again. Shit, I don't know what the hell to do."

"Keep doing it if it feels good. Hide it, that's all. It's nobody's business what you're doing anyway, Leroy."

"Yeah, yeah, that's the way I figure it. I'm just scared someone's gonna find out and throw Craig in jail or beat me to shit. The guys at school roll queers all the time. I ain't up for being blasted to hell, for sure."

"Leroy, you screwed any girls?"

"Yeah, I screwed this blonde whore at the Blue Dog Inn one night. Everybody had a shot at her. I didn't think it was so great. I mean it was okay but it wasn't so great. You been fucking around?"

"Naw, it's harder for girls. I go doin' it and I lose everything, you know. Carrie and Florence would put me in a convent plus the whole damn school would run me to the ground. But I'll do it on the sly, the first chance I get. See, the real problem is getting the boy to shut his mouth. They screw a girl and they got to announce it to the whole friggin' world. I got to find a boy with his tongue cut out or something."

"You ain't worried about getting pregnant?"

"No, I ain't that stupid."

"Do you think I'm a queer?"

"I think you are Leroy Denman, that's what I think. I don't give a flying fuck what you do, you're still Leroy. It's kinda cool that Craig likes you and you get to fly around on that big machine. He sounds nice. And he sounds better than pumping some tired whore, who don't give a shit if you live or die. I mean, Leroy, at least he cares about you. That's got to count for something now, doesn't it?"

"Yeah, but it makes me feel funny inside. Sometimes when I hear songs on the radio, I think that's how I feel about Craig. That scares me a lot more than getting sucked off. What if I'm in love with him for Chris' sake? Have you ever loved anybody?"

"I think I loved Leota, but that was a long time ago."

"See, I told you you were queer."

"Fuck off. Why have you got to label everything? Get off that jag before I bust you one in the mouth."

"That's the way it is. You ain't gonna find many people that think like you so you'd better be ready to hear what they call you when you talk to them the way you talk to me."

"Guess I'll find out for myself, because I ain't shuttin up." Leroy didn't look much better than when we started this conversation. He was fiddling with his fishing pole. "You got something more to say?"

"No."

"Then why are you so God almighty nervous?"

He shifted his weight and stammered, "You said you'd do it if nobody'd tell? I like you better than any girl I ever met and well, I got to find out, you know. I won't tell, I promise I won't tell, if you'll do it with me. Come on, please."

The thought of doing it wasn't shocking, it was that I'd never thought about doing it with ole Leroy. "But Leroy I don't think I feel, uh—romantic about you."

"That don't matter. We're best friends and that's better than all that mush."

"How are we gonna do it without getting caught?"

"We'll go down to the shack back of the lots. Only other person who ever goes there is Ted and he's at work. Come on."

"Okay, it can't be all that bad, I guess." We snuck around the far side of the trailer and went down through the palmetto scrubs to the shack. An old twin-bed mattress that had the stuffing half knocked out of it was on the floor. We checked it for snakes and bugs. Then Leroy whips out his thing and jumps on top of me.

"Leroy, you asshole. Don't you want to take your clothes off?"

"I never did that before."

"Well, I ain't fuckin' unless you take every stitch off. I want to see what I'm getting."

"Okay, okay, I'm taking them off." He tugged at his socks, dawdled with his pants and generally took a very long time. I had my things off in about two seconds.

"Molly, I never saw a girl without her clothes on except in dirty pictures. You look fine. I can see all those little muscles in your stomach. Your stomach is better than mine. Look. You haven't got very big tits though."

"Go by a pair of falsies and play with them."

"It don't matter none," he said getting stuck on his zipper. "I think huge ones are ugly anyway, but all the guys go nuts about them. Can you get this zipper down?"

After a struggle I got his jeans off. He was determined not to take his jockey shorts off so I reached up and pulled them down in one jerk. Leroy gave out a little shriek.

"Quit this foolin around and get on down here."

He snuggled up next to me and lay quietly for a few minutes. Then he gave me a slobbering kiss, he never did get the hang of it but at least he had a hard on. After that he crawled on top of me and gets ready to do his number.

"Leroy, we ought to wait around awhile. One kiss isn't exactly the whole show."

"I thought you said you didn't ever fuck so how come you're telling me what to do? At least, I've done it before." It didn't seem worth it to tell him about Leota so I said, "Okay, do it your way." Leroy huffed and puffed. All those books I'd read said it's supposed to hurt the first time but it didn't hurt at all. In fact, Leroy felt dimly good in there but well, it just wasn't the same as Leota even though that seemed a thousand years ago. If I closed my eyes I could still feel her lips on mine. Even now it gave me a shudder.

Leroy rolled off, exultant. "That was a lot better than that old whore."

I leaned up on one elbow and looked at Leroy with fuzz on his cheeks and small defined muscles already bulging in his back. Well Leroy, I thought, it might have been a lot better than that whore, but you can't hold a candle to Leota. Yeah, maybe

I'm queer. But why would people get so upset about something that feels so good? Me being a queer can't hurt anyone, why should it be such a terrible thing? Makes no sense. But I'm not gonna base my judgment on one little fuck with ole Leroy. We got to do it a lot more and maybe I'll do around twenty or thirty men and twenty or thirty women and then I'll decide. I wonder if I could get twenty people to go to bed with me? Oh it doesn't really matter anyway.

"I am truly glad to know I'm better than a worn-out prostitute." I laughed and threw Leroy back on the mattress. He thought I was going to beat him up and started pleading. "Shut up, stupid, I'm not going to hit you." I kissed him and grabbed his thing. He was in utter shock, "You can't do that."

"Whaddaya mean, I can't do that?"

"Men and women are supposed to close eyes and fuck. You're not supposed to grab me."

"You amaze me. You are for sure getting yourself screwed on rules other people make. I can do whatever I want. I feel like playing with you and I'm gonna do it. Why don't you lie down and shut up. It's kinda fun anyway." He started to protest but I put my arm up to belt him and he laid there quiet as a lamb.

The sun was setting over the flatlands full of sandspurs, lizards, and cockroaches when we headed back for the trailer. "You ain't saying anything, Molly, you promised."

"I'm not breathing one word. Anyway, you got something on me so why worry. I got everything to lose if I rat on you. So don't worry. We'll do it again sometime. And don't worry about Craig, either. You hear me, Leroy? Just do what you damn well please."

Leroy looked at me with grateful eyes and gave me a hug. We got back to the trailer in time for supper. Florence was scurrying around with her apron on, putting food on the tiny table. She asked over the black-eyed peas, "You two been down at the canal all this time? You catch anything down there?"

"Just a couple of queer fish," I said.

Leroy choked on his chicken wing and Florence asked if we wanted more milk.

Sure enough, Leroy flunked eighth grade and had to go to summer school, but then he went on to flunk ninth grade, twice. We saw each other less and less over those three years because I was involved in so many extra-curricular activities that often my Sundays were taken up. It was just as well because Leroy was getting more and more like any other red neck. It got to the point where he thought he owned me, just because we'd do it every now and then. The crowning blow came when he bought a metalflake maroon Bonneville Triumph and I could drive it better than he could. He blew up and told me I really was a dyke and why didn't I just shove off. Craig had left Palm Beach County the year before, and Leroy swore he hadn't had anything like that going on so he was very righteous in his heterosexuality. If that wasn't bad enough he had a girlfriend at school and they were all the time at it so he was unbearable. I told him that he was an asshole plus his points were blasted so he'd better get the bike to the shop. He nearly lost his scrotum and I turned on my heel and marched off.

Aside from Leroy acting like a moron, things were fine. I had gotten invited into all three service clubs at once—Juniorettes, Anchor, and Sinawiks. I thought I was the original hot ticket. I picked Anchor because my two best friends were in there, Carolyn Simpson and Connie Pen. Also, Anchor was the sister club to Wheel Club and I was going out with Clark Pfeiffer, vice-president of Wheel. It seemed like a supreme achievement at the time.

Carolyn was the school Goody Twoshoes. She made me sick ninety percent of the time, but she loved the movies as much as I did, so our bond was seeing every movie in town and then tearing it apart, scene by scene. I began to think maybe I'd be a great film director, although I still hadn't given up the idea of becoming president. Carolyn had deep blue eyes and black hair and was about five feet eight inches tall. She laughed at everything I said but then everyone did that. Underneath it all, she was still school chaplain, so what I could do with Carolyn was limited. On top of that she was a cheerleader, and she was forever at practice out behind the gym concentrating on getting her voice very low. Ft. Lauderdale High's Flying L's prided themselves on their bassthroated cheerleaders. I think they were shooting up on androgen to lengthen their vocal cords. Their voices in unison could drown out all the thousands of the enemy on the other side of the bleachers.

Connie Pen was a different story entirely. A little hefty, like a butterfly swimmer, Connie commanded your attention by her bulk, but she was physically lazy; swimming on the team was the last thing she'd do. She simply ate too much. Her eyes were a clear, warm brown and her hair matched them but the best thing about Connie was that she was totally irreverent. We were made for each other, except that I was physically attracted to Carolyn, and except for the fact that Connie was hyper-heterosexual. She talked about it all the time, a real motor mouth.

All three of us took advanced Latin together, and in our junior year, we applied ourselves to the task of translating the *Aeneid*. Aeneas is a one-dimensional bore. We never could figure out how Virgil got it published, and the tedium of the main character encouraged us to enliven those sultry days in Latin class. The teacher, Miss Roebuck, only added to our energy. Miss Roebuck was from Georgia, and her Latin was Georgian Latin. It was always "all a ya chotaw est" rather than *alea jacta est*. We had heard the rumor from seniors who survived the *Aeneid* that Miss Roebuck would burst into tears when we got to the part where Aeneas leaves Dido. Connie called her "Dildo," of course. So on that day Connie and I decided to cinch Latin for the rest of our high school career. We brought onions hidden in handkerchiefs. Miss Roebuck's voice started to quiver as Dido looked out her window at the de-

parting Trojan. Then at Virgil's giving Dido her
suicidal buildup, Miss Roebuck opened the water-
works. The class tried very hard not to look up
from their texts and trots they were so embarrassed, but Connie and I started sniffling and
showed tears on our cheeks. Carolyn looked at us
in amazement and I flashed the onion at her. Her
Presbyterian morality was offended, but she
couldn't suppress a laugh. Soon the entire classroom was in hysterics which only highlighted our
grief over the Carthaginian queen's plight. Miss
Roebuck looked at us with infinite fondness and
then in her stentorian voice, "Class, most of you
are shamefully, shamefully insensitive. Great lit-
erature and great tragedy are beyond your grasp."
She dismissed the class and called Connie and me
aside. "You girls are true students of the classics."
She patted us on the backs with tears in her eyes
and ushered us out the classroom. Connie and I
became inseparable after that. We concocted one
scheme after another and soon the whole school,
two thousand strong, began to hang on our every
action, word, look. The power was overwhelming.

Our supreme achievement was going back into
the school late at night (we were both in Student
Council and had keys to everything) and putting
a very dead fish in the huge main study hall
ventilator. Classes had to be suspended for one
full day while janitors cleaned out the mess. For
weeks afterward the rooms near main study hall
had the faint reek of rotten fish. Everyone was in
our debt for getting them out of class and no one
told.

However, we came upon a little piece of information that expanded our power beyond the student body to the administration. I became aware of how government really functions.

Saturday night, Connie, Carolyn, and I made a pact that we wouldn't go out with our boyfriends but that we'd go to the movies and get drunk. It took courage for Carolyn to come to that decision, but finally she did with her irrefragable logic which ran that she'd do better to get drunk with the girls and find out how she could handle herself than to do it on a date and risk losing her virginity.

The movie was down at the Gateway so we went to the 7:30 show and sat in the front row. It was a blah movie and Connie wrecked it beyond repair by inserting her own dialogue at appropriate points, such as when Paul Newman meets his boss's wife in the library: "Hello Mrs. So and So, so nice to meet you. Let's fuck." There was one scene in which the wife of a wrinkle zips into Paul Newman's bedroom to try to get him to do it. Connie was having spasms over Newman's bod and I was having spasms over the lady. Connie kept nudging me, "What a bod. What a bod."

I answered, "Yeah, so long and slender and smooth."

"What are you talking about?"

"Huh?"

"Paul Newman's body is not long and slender and smooth, fool."

"Oh."

Paul Newman turned the lady down and it depressed me no end as I was dying to see him take off her slip. I then noticed that Carolyn Simpson slightly resembled the lady in the black slip; they were both tall at any rate. Carolyn took on new stature in my eyes and I started getting that warning signal in my stomach. I had been so busy at school I didn't think about things like that. Godammit, I have to go to this ridiculous movie and my stomach goes into a knot. I'll never be able to look at a black slip again. I was heavy into this vein of thought when the movie at long last ended and we were on our way to Jade Beach.

Jade Beach was an unpatrolled piece of sand between Pompano and Lauderdale-by-the-Sea. It was a well-known do-it place and we picked our way over the bodies to a spot behind a dune. Connie produced a bottle of vodka stolen from her father's bar. We passed it around in mock communion.

Carolyn coughed, "It burns. Why didn't you warn me?"

"You'll get used to it," Connie volunteered.

"Here, gimme that. You know my father finishes off a bottle of this stuff every two days? He drinks it because you can't smell it. His stomach must be rotted to hell by now."

"How come your old man drinks so much, Connie?" Carolyn asked, the spirit of innocence.

"Obviously because he's miserable, dolt. Why else do people drink? He and the old lady fight all the time and I think they're both fucking around. They need the alcohol to lubricate their genitals. You know, they've been dried up by middle age, low horizons, and conformity, blah, blah, blah. That's why my old man drinks."

"Connie, don't say such things about your parents," Carolyn scolded.

"Truth is truth," Connie affirmed.

"Ditto," I belched.

"Do your parents drink and fight, Molly?" Carolyn pressed on.

"Mine? No they're dead and too dumb to fall over." Connie roared and Carolyn tried not to.

"This sounds like 'Youth Wants to Know.' You started this, Carolyn, so fess up about your kin," I said.

"Mother remarried last year so they're still in love. And you know what?"

"What?" we both asked.

"I can hear them in their bedroom doing it." Carolyn's eyes shone with this juicy information.

"You ever done it, Carolyn?" I asked, truly curious.

"No, I'm not going to bed with anyone until I'm married."

"Oh, shit." Connie spit out her vodka on the sand. "You can't be that square."

Carolyn was both hurt and intrigued. She hadn't had sexual encouragement before. "Well, I've fooled around but it's a sin to go all the way before you're married."

"Yes, and I'm a rat's ass," Connie offered.

"Carolyn, you're being a little Victorian. I mean, it doesn't have to be this big deal, you know."

She looked at me after that little rap and fired, "Well, have either of you done it?"

Connie and I looked at each other, took a deep breath, then hesitated. Connie began, "There comes a time in the intercourse of human events when, yes, dear Carolyn, I have done it." She finished her sentence with a grand hand flourish, clutching the dwindling vodka bottle.

"Connie, no," Carolyn breathed, scandalized and delighted.

"Connie, yes," Connie chimed.

"Just the facts, Ma'am," I said, pulling a Jack Webb.

"This you'll never believe. Sam Breem, are you quite geared for that one? Sam Breem. Oh and was he ever a winner, let me tell you. We drove around half the friggin' night, trying to find a motel where you could fuck and not be married. And me with my diaphragm I've never used and had to go to three doctors to get because I'm sixteen years old. Super cool, gang, just super cool. So we get in there, this sharp motel room with coral walls. That's enough to ruin your night right there. So we get in there and Sam tries to be suave about the whole thing. He pours me a drink and we chat a bit. Chat. I was a nervous wreck, you know, first fuck and all that jazz, and he wants to chat . . . and cross his legs like the Hathaway ad in *Esquire* magazine. So we finish the drink, rum and coke, ugh, and he decides it's time to kiss me. So we kiss and after a half hour of dry humping and rolling all over the bed he tries to take my clothes off. Listen honeys, never let them try to take your clothes off because they'll pop your buttons, jam your zippers, and make you look as though you've just come from a rummage sale. After that wrestling match, we get down to doing it and in the middle of it, Sam the Man remembers to ask if I'm protected. Protected —what does he think I am, a five-and-dime with a built in burglar alarm? So I said *yes* and he continues on about his business. It was okay but I can't believe they write songs about first times and people kill themselves over it. I mean really."

Carolyn's eyes were about to bug out of her head, her mouth was dragging in the sand. "Oh, it's supposed to be a beautiful experience. It's supposed to be the most intimate experience a human being can have. You're supposed to share this glorious moment and be physically united and—"

"Carolyn, shut up," I said.

Connie took another swig from the bottle. "Drink up sweeties, one last drop for each of you. Besides which it hurt like hell," she finished.

"That's funny, it didn't hurt me at all," I said. "But I probably busted my cherry on a bicycle seat in second grade or something like that."

"You too," Carolyn stammered.

"Carolyn, I've been diddling off and on since eighth grade with the same tired piece of cock."

Connie gave me a shove and we rolled over in the sand laughing like hyenas, and all the while Carolyn is sitting there in saintly shock.

"So glad to find out there's another honest non-virgin around. The one that cracks me up is Judy Trout. She's been down with everything but the Titanic and she's going around doing her white-lace routine. It's enough to make you vomit." Connie's voice betrayed an edge of bitterness. She hated hypocrisy and Ft. Lauderdale High in 1961 was Hypocrisy U.S.A.

"You mean our Anchor sister, Judy Trout?"

"Carolyn, why don't you take another drink, maybe it will clear your head. You seem to be in a permanent fog," I added. "Maybe being chaplain has disconnected your brain." She seemed hurt by that jab and I got a certain savage pleasure out of it. In fact, I began to get enraged at Carolyn sitting there in her righteousness and with that gorgeous long body.

"We've finished the bottle. I don't suppose anyone else can produce liquor in this desert?" Connie looked mournfully at the bottle.

"There's enough booze on Jade Beach to float the navy, but we'd have to sneak some off a blissful couple when they aren't looking."

"Not worth it, Moll, let's go back."

Getting up, Carolyn stumbled. The vodka hit her like a sledgehammer. She draped her arm around my shoulders and giggled that she needed support. She was perfectly blasted, and at that point I wrote off the fact that her hand kept falling against my breast. Besides, I wasn't stone sober myself.

"Which of us is going to drive?" Connie asked.

"Carolyn loses for sure. I can do it. I'm okay, a little tight, but okay."

"Good," Connie sighed, "because I'm going to look out the car window and dream about Paul Newman's shoulders and eyes. Doesn't he just get to you? Too bad it wasn't him instead of Sam Breem."

I wasn't about to volunteer any information about who was getting to me. "You have to start somewhere. Anyway, nobody starts at the top, right?" I slid behind the wheel and tried to figure out how her damn car worked. I also tried to blank out Paul Newman, the woman in the black slip, and Carolyn's hand on my breast.

We started down AIA and Carolyn zonked out in the back seat. "Hope she doesn't puke," Connie growled.

"Me too, I hate that worse than anything. Blood's a lot better than puke."

At the first traffic light I pulled up next to a '60 blue Chevy Bel Air that looked familiar. "Hey Connie, that car looks like Mr. Beers'."

"It is Mr. Beers. Hey look whose right next to him in the seat, and he's got his arm around her! Mrs. Silver, that's who."

"What!" I pulled up for a better look and saw that it was our esteemed principal and our respected dean of women. Before Connie could slouch down in the front seat I honked and waved.

"Bolt, what the fucking hell are you doing? You wanna cause our expulsion?"

"Just wait. You'll see what I'm doing and thank me for it."

"You're drunk, that's what you are."

"Not a chance."

Mr. Beers and Mrs. Silver looked at us with utter, miserable recognition. The light changed, and he floored it.

"What a Monday this is going to be."

Connie gazed in my direction. "They saw us,

that's for sure. How are we ever going to face them. You and your big mouth."

"Use your smarts. It's not us that has to worry about facing them, it's them that has to worry about facing us. They're the married ones surrounded by the patter of little feet, not us. We're just a couple of high school student leaders out on a drunk."

She put her hand to her lips and thought it over. "You're right. Wow. We hit the jackpot. Think we oughta tell Carolyn?"

"God, no, she nearly had a hemorrhage hearing about our adventures. If her prince, Mr. Beers, turns out to be a philandering toad, it will wreck her for sure."

"Let's not tell anyone else, either. It will be our little secret," Connie laughed.

Once at Carolyn's house we had to sneak her in because her parents were religious and would have shit blue if she'd come in drunk. But we woke up her brat of a sister, Babs. We had to pay the little cherub off to keep her quiet. It was hard to believe they belonged to the same family.

Connie took over the wheel and drove me to the flamingo-pink eyesore next to the railroad tracks. I tiptoed out of the car and whispered goodnight to Connie.

The two of us rendezvoused in the cafeteria before school to make certain our Saturday night experience was confirmed and to reaffirm our vows of secrecy. Right in the middle of homeroom, over the squawk box comes this announcement: "Will Molly Bolt and Connie Pen report to the principal's office following homeroom." We looked at each other with a shiver of apprehension, then pulled ourselves together and went into Main Building, heads high.

I had to go see Mrs. Silver while Connie drew Mr. Beers. Mrs. Silver was maybe forty-five years old and she looked okay except she had a blue rinse on her hair. She greeted me nervously and asked me to sit down.

"Molly, you are one of Ft. Lauderdale High's most outstanding students. You've made straight A's all the way through and you've proven yourself to be a very effective leader. In addition, you're the best female athlete we have. Next year you can expect many awards and hopefully scholarships as I know your family is financially —well, I know you need those scholarships."

"Yes, Ma'am."

"If you would allow me, I'd be happy to write one of your college recommendations and try to help you get a full tuition scholarship."

"Thank you very much, Mrs. Silver. I'd be honored to have you recommend me."

"Do you know what you want to study?"

"I waver between law or film but the only film schools are in New York and California and that's a long way off."

"Well, you think it over and we'll try to work something out. You ought to think about schools like Vassar and Bryn Mawr; they have geographical quotas. With your all-round record, I'm certain you'll make the grade provided that your Board Scores are high and I'm sure they will be."

"I promise to think about it. The Seven Sisters never appealed to me but then I never thought seriously about them."

There was an awkward pause, while Mrs. Silver pushed her useless ink blotter around on her desk pad. "Molly, have you thought about running for student council president next year?"

"I've thought about it, but it looks as though Gary Vogel has it in the bag. Anyway, girls have a hard time getting elected."

"Yes, girls have a hard time in the world, generally."

She looked suddenly beaten, old and worn-out. Mrs. Silver, I'm not going to blow the whistle on you. Damn, damn, you look so unhappy. "If I use my imagination maybe I can come up with something that will beat out Gary Vogel, but you know the student council hasn't set a limit on campaign funds and he's rich."

She blinked and a smile crossed her lips. "Either the spending will be limited or you'll have campaign funds. I promise you that."

"I hope so, Mrs. Silver; it would equalize things." Another pause and then out of nowhere I said, "Mrs. Silver, you don't have to buy me off. I won't tell anyone about last Saturday night no matter what happens. I'm sorry you're upset."

Relief and surprise registered on her face. "Thank you."

I left her office and waited by the trophy case for Connie to barrel out. She emerged five minutes later with a grin all over her round face. "You are looking at the newspaper editor for 1962," she beamed.

"And you are looking at the next student council president."

"Oh wow." Connie shook her head and continued in a low voice, "That poor bastard was shaking when I was in his office. How was she?"

"Same way. I told her I'd keep quiet and she shouldn't worry. What'd you tell him?"

"Same thing in a roundabout way. Looks like we have this school sewed up, doesn't it?"

"Yeah," I said. "Sewed up."

The summer between junior and senior year I worked at the tennis courts. Connie was in Mexico and Carolyn went to Maine to counsel at a multi-denominational Protestant camp. Leroy had passed ninth grade and finally was in tenth. He came down a couple of times on his bike but we didn't do it. I was pretty much done with him that way, especially after the fight we'd had over the bike. Sometimes I felt sorry for Leroy. He followed the herd, like any dumb beast, vaguely realizing he was unhappy. He was impressed when he found out I'd been elected student council president by a landslide vote. But our conversations ran out of gas more frequently and we'd fall back on bikes, cars, and movies. Once he confessed to me in a pathetic voice, "You know, I can talk to you like any regular person. I can't talk to other girls. I pick them up, drive to the movies, go out fucking, and then drive them home. What happens when you get married? I mean, what do people talk about when they're married?"

"Their kids, I guess."

"Maybe that's all they have in common."

And it became increasingly clear that all Leroy and I had in common was a childhood full of ice cream, raisin boxes, and a mattress full of holes. But then I had never thought I had much in common with anybody. I had no mother, no father, no roots, no biological similarities called sisters and brothers. And for a future I didn't want a split-level home with a station wagon, pastel refrigerator, and a houseful of blonde children evenly spaced through the years. I didn't want to walk into the pages of *McCall's* magazine and become the model housewife. I didn't even want a husband or any man for that matter. I wanted to go my own way. That's all I think I ever wanted, to go my own way and maybe find some love here and there. Love, but not the now and forever kind with chains around your vagina and a short circuit in your brain. I'd rather be alone.

Carrie and Florence were scandalized that I had been elected student council president. Carrie had her heart set on me being prom queen and she knew you couldn't be both president and prom queen. She felt I was a traitor to my sex. Florence wasn't so het up about it but she did think it was odd. Her theory was that government was so dirty we should leave it up to the men. I stayed out of the house as much as I could but then I'd been doing that since I could move on my own two legs. Whenever I was home there was always a fight. One night after a huge mouth battle over my cutting my hair, I stormed out of the house and started to get in the car. Carrie ran out the door screeching, "Don't you go taking that car, your father wants to use it." So I got out and slammed the door as hard as I could. Carl came outside and asked me where I wanted to go.

"Nowhere. I just wanted to drive, that's all. Anyplace to get away from our friendly neighborhood harpies."

"Well, you can drive with me."

Carl drove out Sunrise Boulevard and turned left at the beach. Up by Birch State Park we found a quiet spot and got out. He sat on a green bench and looked at the ocean.

"Ocean's really beautiful. I can't believe there's countries on the other side of it and someone over there is sittin' looking at it right as I'm sittin' here now."

"Yeah." I was still pissed.

"I don't think I could live without the ocean. All those years in Pennsylvania. I couldn't go back to that."

"Yeah. I love the ocean too, but I don't know if I'll live by it all the time. Anyway, I don't really like Florida."

"I guess it is kind of a place for old people. Kids don't like to stay where they was raised anyhow so you'll probably move on."

"I want to go where I have a chance. I don't have a chance here. Besides I want to get away from all the people we know. They just get in my way."

"You and your mother are like oil and water. You can't just say 'Yes' to her and go about your business. You have to flare up at her. Pride, girl, pride. If you'd pretend to give in to her you wouldn't have all these fights."

"She's wrong. I give in to her and it confirms her mistakes."

"She's set in her ways. I wouldn't go so far as to say she's all the time wrong."

"I say she's wrong, leastways when it comes to messing with my life she's wrong. She's got to have her own way. No one is telling me what to do. No one. Especially when they're wrong."

"I dunno. Me, I don't like fights, right or wrong. I smile and say 'Yes' to the boss at work and 'Yes' to Carrie and 'Yes' to my folks when they was alive. I slide by."

"I can't do that, Dad."

"I know. You'll pay for it, honey. Tears and bitterness, 'cause you'll be out there fighting all by yourself. Most people are cowards, like me. And if you try to get them to fight they'll turn on you, bad as the people you originally fightin' with. You'll be all alone."

"I'm all alone now. I'm a tenant in that house and that's all I ever was. I got no one but my own sweet self."

Carl looked startled and said, "You got me. I'm your father. You ain't gonna be alone when I'm around."

"Oh Daddy, you never are around." He looked so hurt I could have bitten my tongue off.

"It's that I'm so tired when I come home from work these days. When you was little and I got home you'd be asleep. Then as you grew you'd be outside with the kids. Now I can't seem to work up a head of steam. Some days at work I think I'll go home and eat supper then drive down to school to watch you run the show. Then I sit down and read the paper and fall asleep. I don't get around you much. Too old, I guess—I'm sorry, honey."

"I'm sorry too, Daddy." I stared out at the dark waves and tried not to look him in the face.

"Molly, I'm real proud of the things you been doin' at school. You're something else again, you are. You're gonna go on and be something someday. And you keep on fighting for yourself. Hell, if you can fight Carrie anyone else will be small potatoes." He chuckled and continued, "Do you know where you're gonna go to school and what you're gonna take up?"

"Not yet—the schools I mean. Maybe I'll go to one of those snotty Seven Sisters where the rich brats go or maybe a big city school. Depends on who gives me the best deal. But I know what I want to do, sort of—gonna be law or film directing. Those are the only things I care about."

"You'd make a good lawyer. Nobody can outtalk you, you mix'em up worse than a dog's breakfast. But now this director business, I dunno. You gotta go to Hollywood, don't you? That's a bad place, they say."

"I don't know. The studios are falling apart, that much I know. Seems like there ought to be some openings somewhere—new companies and stuff. But I got to get the skills first. There aren't any women directors, so I will have a fight for sure and law, well, I know I have a good shot at it. But I'd rather make movies than talk to some sleepy jury."

"Then make movies. You only got one life so do what you want."

"That's how I figure it."

"What about gettin' married?"

"I'm never doing it. Period."

"I could see that coming. You wouldn't look too hot on the other side of an apron and between us, it'd kill me to see you buckle under to anyone, especially a husband."

"Well, don't worry about it 'cause it'll never happen. Besides, why should I buy a cow when I get the milk for free? I can go out and screw anytime I damn well please."

He laughed. "People are silly about sex. But if you'll take a word of advice from your old man— do it all you want but be quiet about it." There was a strange sadness in his voice; he paused and bent over to make a circle in the sand. "Molly, I haven't done much good with my life and now it's almost gone. I'm fifty-seven. Fifty-seven. I can't get used to it. When I think of myself sometimes I think I'm still sixteen. Funny ain't it? To you I'm an old fogey but I can't quite believe I'm old. Listen to me," his voice got stronger, "you go on and do whatever you want to do and the hell with the rest of the world. Learn from your old man. I never did a goddamned thing and now I'm too old to do anything. All I got is dead dreams and a mortgage on that house with ten years left to pay. I worked my whole life and all I got to show is that square, pink house sitting next to the railroad tracks with other square houses. Shit. You damn the torpedoes and full speed ahead, kid; don't listen to nobody but your own self."

"Dad, you've been watching those war movies again." And I gave him a big hug and a kiss on his gray salty stubble.

The middle of July was hot. I had returned from Girls' State triumphant as governor. Carrie and Florence mumbled there'd be no living with me now. Carl went to work and told everyone he saw that his daughter was going to be the real governor someday. One night shortly after I came back from Tallahassee, Carl and I watched *Peter Gunn* on the tube. We took bets on who was the villain and Carl won because it was a repeat. He didn't tell me that he'd seen it before until after the show and he laughed his way into the bedroom.

I went to bed around eleven and fell asleep with palm leaves rustling outside. Palm fronds sound like—rain—it's a soothing sound. I was jolted out of a deep sleep by someone clawing at my face. Fingernails scratched at my throat. The room was jet black but for an eerie red light from outside flickering through the drawn Venetian blinds. I could see another shape on the bed pulling at whoever was clawing me. Gradually my eyes focused and I saw that it was Carrie who was attacking me, making strange noises.

She's gonna kill me. She's off her nut and she's trying to strangle me. Then she started wailing at the top of her lungs, "Wake up, wake up. Carl's dead. Wake up, Molly, your father's dead." Florence had her hands full getting Carrie off me. She confirmed the report, "He's out there in the living room if you want to see him before they roll him away. Go now 'cause the ambulance is here and so is the doctor." I threw on my robe and ran into the living room with the big mirror that had flamingoes painted on it. There under the mirror in front of the door was Carl's body. His eyes were staring straight up into mine and he was all blue in the face.

"Why's he blue?"

The doctor answered, "Heart attack. It happened very suddenly. He had time to warn Carrie and he said he thought it was his heart, then boom, he was gone."

The ambulance men came in and looked at me curiously in my robe. Made no difference to them that my father had died. I was another piece of sixteen-year-old ass in a bathrobe. The doctor told me to put Carrie on tranquilizers she was so whacked out. All that night even though we crammed her full of pills she kept waking up and crying, "What day is this? Where's my Carl?" Then she'd call him like she was calling the cat, "Carl, oh Carl, come hereee." There was no use trying to get back to sleep, so Florence and I stayed up the whole night and discussed funeral arrangements. Florence was looking at me with the searching eye, waiting for me to falter or cry. If I'd cried, she would have told me to pull myself together for Carrie's sake. Since I didn't cry, she accused me of being heartless and not truly loving Carl because he wasn't my natural father. She upbraided me for being adopted and how adopted kids got no true feelings for their parents. I was wordless. I had nothing to say to that woman. Let her think what she damn well pleased. People like that, I don't give a shit what they think.

The funeral was set for Sunday. When we went down to Zimmer's Funeral Home with Carl's clothes we discovered that Carl wasn't there. We called every funeral home in the city trying to track down his remains and found him at Bolt's Funeral Home. Since his last name was Bolt the ambulance drivers got mixed up and took him to the wrong parlor. Didn't matter to them that they'd made a mistake, they charged us twice anyway.

After the service we got in the big, white Continental to drive out to the cemetery and Carrie recovered her sense of humor long enough to say, "Well, this is the first time I got to ride in such a rich car. Seem's like someone's got to die before you can ride in a Lincoln Continental." She giggled and Florence looked at her as though she'd been deranged by the sorrow. I thought it was pretty funny myself. For all our fights, there was no getting around the fact that Carrie wasn't fooled by show and she regarded most of the world around her as a show for the rich at the expense of the poor.

Loneliness settled over the pink house with Carl's death. Carrie cried nearly every day right up until I went back to school. I tried staying around for awhile to make her feel better, but all we did was fight. We'd fight about the funeral, fight about me not carrying on over it, fight about me working at the tennis courts instead of as a file clerk. I gave up on staying home and went out all the time. Then we fought about me leaving her in the house with her buckets of misery.

Two weeks after school started, I came home around five and changed my clothes to go back later for a meeting. Florence had succeeded in prying Carrie from the house and took her window shopping at the new Britt's store. I was sitting in the bright yellow kitchen reading Virginia Woolf's

Orlando, laughing my head off, when I looked up at the clock and noticed it was five-thirty. I jumped up and put on the coffee pot. The deep rust colors swirled through the clean water when I looked out the jalousie door and realized Carl was never coming home again. I felt so stupid and desolate, putting on the pot so he'd have fresh coffee after work. I sat down and tried to read *Orlando* again, but I couldn't focus on the page. I stood up and went back into Carrie's bedroom. Carl had a drawer in the huge, brown old dresser with the gray linoleum top. The little thin drawer cherished a handful of old pearly penknives, a red and silver palm size cigarette case from the thirties and a worn, oval ring with Athena's head carved in the sardonyx. A whole human life is gone. A wonderful, laughing life and all that's left is this handful of used-up goods, and they're not even quality stuff.

The limping '52 Plymouth rolled into the carport and I heard those two get out, each one grumbling to the other that she didn't need help. I zoomed back into the kitchen and opened my book. Florence right off noticed that my eyes were red and my nose was running.

"What's wrong with you?" she demanded.

"I was reading this sad book, that's all."

Carrie snorted that all I ever did was read sad books and I was going to ruin my eyes. "You all the time got your nose in a book. A bookworm, that's what you are, straining those eyes since a baby on up. You won't listen to me. No, you never listen to me. I tell you for your own good you got to stop this reading so much. Besides that it ain't good for your brains as well as your eyes to be reading all the time. Makes things percolate over-time. Ruin your health sure as I'm standing here talking to you. Molly, do you hear me!"

"Yes, Mom."

She opened a big white bag with Thank You written on it in script and showed me a wilderness of plastic flowers. "They're for your father's grave. They'll last longer than real ones. It'll look pretty when people drive by."

"They're pretty. Excuse me, I gotta go back to school."

As I started out the door I heard Florence say to Carrie, "That girl of yours is crazy. She don't cry over her father's death, but she sits here and cries over some dern book."

Senior year was a victory. Connie and I never had to go to class if we didn't want to. Mr. Beers wrote us blue freedom slips at a moment's notice. The only class we condescended to attend was Advanced English with Mrs. Godfrey. She was such a great teacher that we didn't mind learning Middle English to read Chaucer. Carolyn was in the class also. The three of us sat in the front row and fought it out between us for the highest grade.

Carolyn was captain of the cheerleaders and she usually showed up in the lunchroom in her uniform with blue tassels on her white boots. Connie and I scoffed at such a thing as cheerleading, but Carolyn was the social leader of the school because of it. The three of us also dated three boys who were close friends. Whenever we were seen with our respective boyfriends, we paid the usual fondling attention to him demanded by rigid high-school society but in truth, none of the three of us gave a damn about any of them. They were a convenience, something you had to wear when you went to school functions, like a bra. Carolyn was becoming tighter than a violin string because Larry kept pushing her to sleep with him. Connie and I told her to go ahead and get it over with because we were sick of hearing her bitch about Larry grabbing her boob at 12:20 A.M. every Saturday night. Besides Connie and I were both doing it with our boyfriends with no harmful side effects. No one was supposed to know of course, but everyone did in that behind-the-hand manner. All this overt heterosexuality amused me. If they only knew. Our boyfriends thought they were God's gift because we were sleeping with them but they were so tragically transparent that we forgave them their arrogance.

Carolyn decided, again with her relentless logic, that if we won the football game against Stranahan, she'd do it with Larry. We creamed them. Carolyn's face walking off the field of honor was not the usual bright cherry red from screaming her lungs out but an ashen and drawn white. Connie and I went over to her to bolster her. Then the three of us went back to the locker room to wait for our dates—all Princeton haircuts, Weejun shoes, and Gold Cup socks. Clark came out with a gash on his cheek and wanted sympathy. I told him he was a football hero, which he was, having made two touchdowns. Connie's Douglas lumbered out (right tackles tend to grow large) and she told him he was a football hero. Larry stumbled coming out of the door he was in such a rush to see Carolyn. She didn't have time to tell him he was a football hero because he gave her a bone-crushing kiss which was a rerun of an Errol Flynn movie and picked her up bodily, placing her in his Sting Ray convertible. Carolyn nervously waved good-bye and we all waved back. Then the four of us climbed into Doug's car and headed for Wolfie's for endless talk about this missed tackle and that fine block interspersed with bananas and hot fudge sundaes.

The next morning the phone rang around 9:00 A.M. It was Carolyn. "I have to talk to you right now. Are you awake?"

"I guess I am if I answered the phone."

"I'm coming over and we can have breakfast at the Forum, okay?"

"Okay."

Fifteen minutes later Carolyn arrived looking paler than usual. As I slid in the front seat of the car I asked, "How is Ft. Lauderdale High's newest harlot?"

She grimaced. "I'm all right, but I have to ask you some questions so I know I did it right."

Over eggs that looked as though the chickens rejected them, she began, "Is it always such a mess? You know, when I stood up all this stuff ran down my leg. Larry said it was sperm. It was so disgusting I nearly barfed."

"You get used to it."

"Yech. And another thing—what am I supposed to do during all this, lie there? I mean, what do you really do? There they are on top of you sweating and grunting and it's not at all like I thought."

"Like I said, you get used to it. It isn't very mystical if that's what you're waiting for. I'm not an expert or anything, but different people are different. Larry may not be the hottest lay in the world, so don't base your judgment on his one performance. Anyway, they're supposed to get technically better as they grow older. We hit them at that awkward age, I guess."

"That's not what the medical book says. It says they reach their prime at eighteen and we reach ours at thirty-five. How's that for timing? It's all so ridiculous. You and Connie must think I'm a real spastic."

"No, you take it too seriously, that's all."

"Well, it is serious."

"No, it isn't. It's a big dumb game and it doesn't mean anything at all unless you get pregnant, of course. Then it means you're screwed."

"I'll try. Hey, you want to go drinking Friday?"

"Sure. What about Connie?"

"She has to go to some journalism conference in Miami for the weekend."

"Okay, so it will be the two of us."

Friday night we went to the children's playground at Holiday Park. No one came there late at night, and the police patrols were too busy beating the bushes and their own meat to harass the playground. I didn't really like drinking so I took a few swings to make it look good, but Carolyn got blasted. She slid down the fireman's pole, played on the swings and discarded various pieces of her clothing at each go round. When she got down to her underwear, she made a beeline for the grounded blue jet and crawled in the open tail to the fuselage. She stayed in there making airplane sounds and showed no sign of giving up her piloting. I crawled in after her. It was a tiny, narrow space so I had to lie down next to her.

"Carolyn, maybe you should join the Air Force when you graduate. You've got the sound effects down pat."

"Whoosh." Then she leaned up on one elbow and asked in a coy voice, "How does Clark kiss you?"

"On the lips, where else? What do you mean how does he kiss me? What a dumb question."

"Want me to show you how Larry kisses?"

Without waiting for my sober answer she grabbed me and laid the biggest kiss on my face since Leota B. Bisland.

"I doubt he kisses that way." She laughed and kissed me again. "Carolyn, do you know what you're doing?"

"Yes, I'm giving you kissing lessons."

"I'm very grateful but we'd better stop." We'd better stop because one more kiss and you're going to get more than you bargained for, lady. Or maybe that's what you are bargaining for?

"Ha." She dropped another one on me this time with her entire body pressed against mine. That did it. I ran my hands along her side, up to her breast, and returned her kiss with a vengeance. She encouraged this action and added a few novelties of her own like nibbling my sensitive ears. By this time I began to worry about being in the tail end of an old blue jet in the middle of the children's playground in Holiday Park. Carolyn had no such worries and threw off what was left of her clothing. Then she started taking off mine and tossed them up in the cockpit. If I was worried, I got over it. All I could think about was making love with Carolyn Simpson, head cheerleader and second-year chaplain of Ft. Lauderdale High School—and a cinch for prom queen. We were in that plane half the night coming in the wild blue yonder. I know we broke the sound barrier. Eventually, the sky began to lighten and the air became chilly. I thought it was time to go. "Let's get out of here."

"I don't want to get out, I want to stay in here for ten years and play with your breasts."

"Come on." I reached up and got her underwear and my clothes. Then I backed out of the plane and collected her dew-covered bermuda shorts, Villager blouse, and white, worn-out sneakers. Shivering, we ran to the car.

"Are you hungry?" I asked.

"For you."

"Carolyn, you are so goddamned corny. Let's go to the 'Egg and You' and get something good."

I ordered two breakfasts for all the energy I burned up, and Carolyn had bacon and eggs.

"Molly, you won't tell will you? I mean we could really get in trouble."

"No, I'm not telling but I hate lying. It seems pretty impossible that anyone would ask such a thing, so the coast is clear."

"I hate to lie too, but people will say we're lesbians."

"Aren't we?"

"No, we just love each other, that's all. Lesbians look like men and are ugly. We're not like that."

"We don't look like men, but when women make love it's commonly labeled lesbianism so you'd better learn not to cringe when you hear the word."

"Have you ever done that before?"

"When I was in sixth grade but that was about seven centuries ago. Did you?"

"At camp this summer. I thought I'd die from the fright but she was so terrific, this other counselor. I never thought of her as a lesbian, you know. We spent all our time together and one night she kissed me, and we did it. I didn't stop to think about it at the time, it felt too good."

"Do you write her?"

"Sure. We'll try to go to the same college. Molly, do you think you can love more than one person at a time? I mean, I love you and I love Susan."

"I guess so. I'm not jealous, if that's what you're after."

"Kinda. You want to know something else? It's a lot better than doing it with Larry. I mean there's no comparison, you know?"

"That I know." We laughed and ordered two hot fudge sundaes at 6:00 in the morning.

Carolyn started waiting for me in the lunchroom and paying all kinds of attention to me. She forgot to pay attention to Larry or Connie. Larry didn't mind as long as he got his weekend fuck, but Connie was more sensitive. Because of it, I tried to spend more time with Connie, which made Carolyn mad. The times the three of us were together became more and more strained until I began to feel like a bone between two dogs. We were the witches for the English class's production of *Macbeth* and during rehearsal I tried to explain to Carolyn what I thought was happening and that she should cool it. She burst out with, "Are you sleeping with Connie?"

Connie who was sitting on the other side of a cardboard rock popped her head over the top and said, "What?!"

This is it. Now what do I do? "Carolyn, that's a stupid thing to say. No, I am not sleeping with Connie, but I do love her. She's my best friend and you'd better get used to it." Carolyn began to cry.

Connie looked at me in amazement, and I shrugged my shoulders. "Molly, why would she think we're sleeping together? What's going on?"

"Connie." Pause. What the flying fuck do I say now? "Connie, there's no use trying to lie about it. Carolyn and I have been sleeping together. End of sentence. She got jealous I guess. I don't know." I turned to Carolyn, "Anyway, what the hell are you jealous about, you're the one with Susan, not me. It makes no sense."

Carolyn started to offer an answer through a sniffle but Connie, recovering from shock, beat her to it. "I want to make certain I've got this right. You make love with Carolyn?"

"Yes, I make love with Carolyn. Carolyn makes love with me. I make love with Clark and Carolyn makes love with Larry. All we need is a circular bed and we can have a gang bang. Christ."

"Do the boys know?"

"Of course not. Nobody knows but you. You know what would happen if it leaked out."

"Yeah, everybody would call you queer, which you are, I suppose."

"Connie!" Carolyn shrieked. "We are not queer. How can you say that? I'm very feminine, how can you call me a queer? Maybe Molly, after all she plays tennis and can throw a football as far as Clark, but not me."

Carolyn was dropping her beads, all right. I tried to pretend I didn't know she'd run a number like that when cornered, but I knew it inside. A delicate whiff of hate curled round my nostrils. I'd like to bust her feminine head.

"What does Molly's tennis have to do with it?" Connie was becoming increasingly confused.

"You know, lesbians are boyish and athletic. I mean Molly's pretty and all that but she's a better athlete than most of the boys that go to this school, and besides she doesn't act like a girl, you know? I'm not like that at all. I just love Molly. That doesn't make me queer."

Quiet anger was in Connie's voice as she faced Carolyn. "Well, I'm about fifteen pounds overweight, hefty is what I believe it's called, plus I don't remember that I've ever cooed and giggled in true female fashion, so why don't you come right out and call me a dyke too if that's how your mind is misfunctioning?"

Carolyn was genuinely stunned. "Oh, I never meant that about you. You're just straightforward. Anyway, you're lazy, that's why you're fat. The last thing you are is athletic. You're the career-woman type."

"Carolyn, you make me sick." I threw off my witch's tatters and headed for the auditorium door.

"Molly!" Carolyn screamed.

Connie took off her costume and came out after me. "Where are you going?"

"I don't know, mostly I want to get away from Miss Teenage America in there."

"I've got the car, let's go to the park."

We drove over to Holiday Park and positioned ourselves in the cockpit of the blue jet. I didn't bother to tell Connie about my last time in the jet.

"Do you think you're a queer?"

"Oh great, you too. So now I wear this label 'Queer' emblazoned across my chest. Or I could always carve a scarlet 'L' on my forehead. Why does everyone have to put you in a box and nail the lid on it? I don't know what I am—polymorphous and perverse. Shit. I don't even know if I'm white. I'm me. That's all I am and all I want to be. Do I have to be something?" Connie looked down at her hands and her eyebrows wrinkled over her eyes. "Come on, Connie, what's on your mind?"

"No, you don't have to be anything. I'm sorry I asked you if you were a queer. But this is a big jolt. Things your mother didn't tell you and all that. I guess I'm square, or maybe I'm scared. I don't think you or anyone else should wear a label and I don't understand why who you sleep with is so Goddamned important and I don't understand why I'm all strung out over this. All this time I thought I was this progressive thinker, this budding intellectual among the sandspurs, now I find out I'm as shot through with prejudice as the next asshole. I cover them up with layers of polysyllables." She inhaled and continued, "It wrecked me when you said you were sleeping with Carolyn—*me*, Miss Sarcasm of Ft. Lauderdale High, Miss Fake Sophisticate." I started to say something, but she kept on. "I'm not through, Molly, I don't know if I can be your friend anymore. I'll think about it every time I see you. I'll be nervous and wonder if you're going to rape me or something."

Now it was my turn to be shocked. "That's crazy. What do you think I do, run around panting at every female I see? I'm not going to leap on you like a hyperthyroid ape. Goddammit!"

"I know that. I *know* that, but it's in my head. It's me, not you. I'm sorry. I really am sorry." She swung her leg over and climbed down from the cockpit. "Come on, I'll take you home."

"No. It's not far. I want to walk it."

She didn't look up. "Okay."

That night Carolyn called and filled my ear with four thousand sugary apologies. I told her to shut up and I didn't give a shit what she thought. She could take her prom queen tiara and shove it up her ass.

School was buzzing with the breakup of the gleesome threesome, but none of us spoke so the gossips had to concoct their own stories. One widely accepted was Missy Barton's theory that Connie wanted to sleep with Clark and I wouldn't stand for it. She explained Carolyn's behavior by saying she was torn between the two of us. When

I regained my sense of humor, I thought it was pretty funny but it also made me green around the edges, people are so stupid. Sell them shit in a red cellophane package and they'd buy it.

I was becoming more and more isolated in the splendor of my office. It was a tiring little game once the glamor of being student council president wore off. I longed to return to the potato patch and raise hell with kids who didn't know the difference between Weejuns and Old Maine trotters. But those kids grew up and wore tons of eye-makeup, irridescent pink fingernail polish and scratched each other's eyes out over the boy with the metalflake, candy apple red '55 Chevy with four on the floor. There was no place to go back to. No place to go to. College was going to be like high school, only worse. But I gotta go. I don't get that degree and I'm another secretary. No thanks. I got to get it and head for a big city. Got to hang on. That's what Carl told me once, you got to hang on. It would be nice to talk to Carl. God, it would be nice to talk to someone who wasn't fucked up.

One week before graduation a colorful event rocked the school. Someone had snuck into the girls' shower room before first period gym and unscrewed the shower heads, putting in powdered dyes. Sixty girls had first period gym and the first twenty or so in the showers came out red, yellow, green or blue. The stuff didn't wash off either. That Saturday night as diplomas were handed out it gave me a certain degree of pleasure to notice that Carolyn resembled a consumptive movie-set Indian and Connie looked definitely blue.

When I was handed my diploma, I received a standing ovation from my constituency and a hug from Mr. Beers. When the noise ebbed, he said in the humming microphone, "There's our governor in twenty years." Everyone cheered again and I thought Mr. Beers was as silly or maybe as kind as Carl, who used to tell everyone at work the same thing.

Gainesville, Florida, is the bedpan of the South. Positioned in north central Florida it has scrub pines, Spanish moss, and blood clots of brick institutional buildings. It's the home of the University of Florida. The only reason I went there was because they gave me a full scholarship plus room and board. Duke, Vassar, and Radcliffe offered smaller packages and having no money, my choice was determined by material considerations. Carrie and Florence put me on the Greyhound bus which pulled up behind the Howard Johnson's and took off to pull up behind other Howard Johnsons throughout the state. The bus ride took twelve hours, but finally I arrived and took my first look at the dismal town. With my one suitcase sporting a Girls' State sticker firmly in hand, I walked to the dorm.

The university placed me in Broward Hall,

known on campus as the Bay of Pigs. But it was
free, so I endured it. On that first day I discovered
my roommate, a pre-med from Jacksonville, Faye
Raider. Since I had scribbled pre-law on my entrance forms, the administration probably thought
it would be a good match. It was, but not for
reasons of studiousness. Faye and I discovered a
common bond for disruption and we lost no time
in establishing a system of payoffs to the building
guards, so we could get in and out of the basement
windows after the dorm doors had been locked to
protect our virginity from the night air. Faye
pledged Chi Omega because her mother was a
Chi O back in 1941 and I pledged Delta Delta
Delta because they, like the university, promised
to pay for everything—dirty rush. Faye said she
pledged a sorority to please her mother, whose
only joy in life was the Jacksonville alumnae
association, and I pledged because campus politics
demanded it. This way all my election costs would
be footed jointly by the sorority and the party to
which the sorority belonged, University Party.
I ran for freshman representative and won. Faye
was campaign manager, which Tri-Delta considered a stroke of political brilliance because it
helped unite the houses of Tri-Delta and Chi
Omega, who together dominated the remaining
eleven sororities on campus. Faye and I laughed
at the solemnity with which all this was greeted
by our "sisters" and spent our free hours together
crossing the county line for liquor, bringing it
back to the dorm, watering it slightly and selling
it at a higher price.

We both hated the university with its dull

agricultural majors, grim business majors, and all the girls running around in trench coats with art history books tucked under their left armpits. Faye confessed she didn't really care about being a doctor, but she'd be damned if she'd sit in humanities courses with all those bubbling girls who wore circle pins on their round collars. Her father bought her a 190SL Mercedes to encourage her to study, and he had a habit of sending fat checks in the mail every two weeks. Faye was the spirit of generosity maybe because she didn't know what money was worth, but I loved her for it whatever her motive. She cast one glance at my tiny wardrobe and marched me off to the best store in town and blew three hundred dollars on clothes. To spare my pride she announced she wasn't going to be seen with a roomie who wore the same shirt every other day. I think I was a curiosity to Faye. She couldn't fathom my ambition, but then Faye couldn't fathom poverty.

It was against the rules, of course, but Faye had a tiny icebox hidden in her closet where she kept mixers, olives, and cream cheese. She hid the liquor in shoe boxes. I didn't figure out that Faye was on her way to becoming a late adolescent alcoholic until the middle of October. I asked her why she drank so much but she told me not to go moral on her so I dropped it. Her grades began to sink, and she cut classes more and more frequently. Luckily for me, I never needed to study much to get my grades, because Faye would have no part of studying for herself or anybody else. At nine o'clock each night if we were still in the dorm, Faye would run out in the hall with a huge cowbell, beat on it with a drumstick and yell, "Study, study all you brownnosers." Then she'd sail back in her room and have another drink.

Chi Omega worried about their new pledge when Faye showed up at the dinner for President Reich and veered up to him mumbling, "Hi ya, prex, how ya hangin'?" In an effort to steer her toward the paths of righteousness, she had to have an hour-long heart-to-heart with her big sister, Cathy, once a week. Faye fumed that it was lay psychiatry and offended her new-sprung professional ethics. One Thursday after a session she came back to our room and slammed the door.

"Bolt, I blew it. I just fucking blew it. I told my Goddamn big sistershit that I'm pregnant and need an abortion. Her milk-white face curdled right in front of me. She promised not to tell anyone but I bet dollars to donuts she opens her yap. Will my mother be pissed!"

"Are you sure you're pregnant?"

"Yes, I am Goddamn fucking sure. Enough to make you vomit, isn't it?"

"Where can we get an abortion?"

"I know a guy in med school who will do it. But I have to give him $500. Can you believe $500 to scrape a tiny bit of gook from my insides?"

"Do you think he's safe?"

"Who knows?"

"Well, when are we doing it?"

"Tomorrow night. You're driving me there, cookie."

"Okay. Did you tell Cathy you were going tomorrow?"

"No. At least I had sense enough not to spill that. I don't even know why I told her in the first place. It was on my mind and it popped out. Stupid."

The next evening we left the dorm at nine and drove out west of the town. We pulled in the driveway of the med student's trailer and Faye climbed out.

"I'm coming with you."

"No, you're not. You stay here and wait."

It seemed hours and I was so nervous I threw up. The whole thing was creepy and the Spanish moss in the night looked like ragged fingers of death coming to get me. All I could think of was Faye in there on some kitchen table with him doing God knows what. I thought maybe I should go in there, but then suppose I barge in at the critical moment and he punches a hole in her or something. Eventually Faye wobbled out. I ran out of the car to help her.

"Faysie, are you all right?"

"Yeah, I'm all right. A little weak."

As we neared the dorm I turned out the lights and pulled into the macadam parking lot. We walked slowly back to the basement window that was permanently unlocked at the price of ten dollars per week to the guard. I lifted Faye through because it was high up. As I dropped to the other side I noticed blood oozing down her leg. "Faye, you're bleeding. Maybe we should go to a real doctor."

"No. He told me I might bleed a little. It's okay. Shut up about it or you'll make me think about it." We started up the four flights of stairs to our room and Faye was going painfully slow. "I'm so Goddamned weak this is gonna take a fucking hour."

"Put your arms around my neck and I'll carry you up."

"Molly, you crack me up. I weigh one thirty-five and you must weigh about a hundred."

"I'm very strong. Come on, this is no time to pull a weight watchers. Put your arms around my neck."

She leaned on me and I picked her up. "My hero," she laughed.

I cut classes the next two days to hang around the room in case Faye needed me. She recovered in record time and by Saturday was ready for another liquor-sodden weekend. "I'm going over to Jacksonville to raise hell."

"Don't be an asswipe, Faye. Take it easy this weekend."

"If you're so worried you can come along and play nurse. We can stay at my house and come back Sunday night. Come on."

"Okay, but promise me you won't pick up some stud and bust open your stitches or whatever you've got up there."

"You crack me up."

We started out at a bar near Jacksonville University, black walls, day-glo paint on them and a huge sea-turtle shell here and there. An enormous basketball player bought us drinks and insisted on asking me to dance. My nose hit his navel and I got cramps in my arches from dancing so long on my toes. We left there and headed toward the inner city. "I'm gonna take you to a wild bar, Molly, so gear yourself."

The bar was Rosetta's, named after the owner who walked around with a black lasagna hairdo teased up nearly a foot with chopsticks stuck in it at various angles. Rosetta smiled at us as we came in and demanded our I.D.'s. They were fake, of course, but we passed checkpoint charlie and went over to a table in the corner. As we sat down, I glanced in the direction of the dance floor and noticed that the men were dancing with each other and the women were dancing with other women. I had a sudden urge to clap my hands in frenzied applause, but I suppressed it because I knew no one would understand.

"Faye, how'd you find this place?"

"I get around, Toots."

"Are you gay?"

"No, but I like gay bars. They're more fun than straight ones, plus there's no jocks to paw at you. I thought I'd bring you here for a little treat."

"Thought you'd shock me, right?"

"I don't know. I just thought it would be fun."

"Let's have fun then. Come on, smartass, how'd you like to dance?"

"Bolt, you crack me up. Who the hell is going to lead?"

"You are because you're taller than I am."

"Wonderful, I can be a butchess."

Once on the terrazzo dance floor, we had a hard time keeping our balance because Faye was laughing uproariously. Every two steps she mangled my sandaled foot. Then in a burst of concentration, she gave me a Fred Astaire twirl and made use of her cotillion training. As the final strains of Ruby and the Romantics died down, we started for our table to be intercepted by two young women on the other side of the dance floor.

"Excuse me. Don't you all go to Florida and live in Broward?"

Faye volunteered the information. Then the short one asked us if we'd come to their table for a drink. We agreed to that and trotted back to our corner table to retrieve our drinks.

"Molly, if that little one tries to pick me up, you tell her we're going together. Okay?"

"Instant marriage, is it? In that case, I'll do anything for my wife."

"Thanks, dearie, I'll do the same for you. Remember we're the hottest couple since Adam and Eve. Wrong metaphor—since Sappho and whoever. Come on."

The women's names were Eunice and Dix. They were in Kappa Alpha Theta and came here on weekends under the pretense that their boyfriends lived in Jacksonville but really to escape the prying eyes of their loving sorority sisters. Dix, the little one, was very busy cruising Faye. Faye was worth cruising. She had jet black hair and white porcelain skin that set off light hazel eyes—a Southern belle gone co-ed. I was uncertain about bar etiquette—I didn't know if I was supposed to ask people to dance, buy them drinks or even ask them about themselves, especially since people only gave you their first names. Eunice offered that she was a physical therapy major and Dix was in English. They'd been going together for almost a year and a half.

"How nice," Faye drawled, and I practically strangled on my drink. Faye was singularly unimpressed with any display of romanticism, be it homosexual or common garden variety heterosexual. Dix and Eunice were beyond sarcasm and thought Faye had given them the blessed sign of approval. Thanks to that we got the entire scenario of their love. How they met in math class, how long it took them to get into bed, and so forth. Dix became more animated with every drink; soon she leaned over to confide in us, "You'll never guess what happened to us when we lived in Jennings and had straight roommates."

"I can't wait. Do tell," Faye answered.

"Well, we usually made love in Eunice's room because her roomie had a night class. So one night I'm over there and well, you know I was— uh—I was going down on her and we heard her roomie's voice coming down the hall. Honey, I didn't know whether to go blind, shit, or run for my life. Luckily we had locked the door, so I started to pull away when my braces got caught in Eunice's hair. There was her roommate knocking on the door bellowing and there I was stuck in an incriminating position. No time to be gentle, I yanked myself away. Eunice released this blood-curdling yell and her roommate is outside fumbling with the key in the door screaming someone's trying to murder Eunice. I ran into the closet, Jane got the door open, and half the hall marched in after her to see the corpse. Eunice pulled the covers up over herself, sweaty and frantic, and tried to look in pain—which she was. Jane wants to know what happened. Eunice lied that she had mistakenly locked the door and when she took a nap, her back locked on her. The yell was when she tried to get up to open the door. Then the whole crew of dollies wants to carry Eunice to the infirmary. You shoulda seen Eunice talking herself out of that one. Oh this thing happens every now and then. It would go away overnight. God knows how long it took her to get the room cleared out, and I had to stay in that ratty closet until her roommate went to sleep. Then I tiptoed out and got back to my own dorm, after hours, so I had hell to pay for that."

We laughed since it was expected of us and I was grateful that Dix was so talkative, because if she'd asked me anything I didn't know what I'd say.

Eunice turned to Faye. "How long have you two been going together?"

"Since September when we discovered we were roommates."

"And you didn't know each other before school?" Dix asked.

"No," Faye answered. "It was love at first sight."

"Had either of you been gay before college?" Eunice probed, fascinated with our storybook romance.

This time I beat Faye to the punch. "Faye wasn't but I was."

Faye looked at me suppressing a giggle, thinking I had added a new twist to her fairy tale.

"How long did it take you to seduce her?" Dix pressed on.

"Oh, about one week."

"Yeah, I was an easy lay."

We stayed at the bar for another hour exchanging information about what professor to miss, who else was gay, etc. Faye gracefully extracted us by saying we had to get up early in the morning to go shopping with her mother. On the way home Faye was in hysterics over who was gay in the various sororities. We pulled into the driveway of an imitation colonial mansion overlooking the St. John's river. The inside of the house looked like window cases for a furniture store. Faye's mother had one room in colonial plush, another in Mediterranean, and another in French provincial. Everything was color coordinated and I expected the price tags to still be hanging from the goods. Faye's room was *Seventeen* gone raunchy. Her twin beds had matching orange bedspreads and curtains. A black shag rug wilted between the two beds and the vanity groaned under the weight of all the perfumes and other paraphernalia of female disguise. Faye took off her clothes, threw them on the floor, and flopped into bed. "I am fucking sober. Sober! Weren't those two funny? Wait until we see them at the next Panhellenic pissy tea. That oughta be rich."

"Yeah, but they were sweet in a square, old-fashioned way."

"I suppose but I can't stand it when people get all moonie about each other."

"That's because you've never been in love. You haven't got a heart, Faysie, only a pericardium."

"Thanks."

"Oh, I'm only teasing you. I can't stand all that romantic crap either especially when they play footsie under the table. Gawd. But everybody does it, straight or gay. It turns me off—maybe I'm not either one."

"Even if I fall in love I'm not degenerating into that diddleshit." Faye looked out her window over the dark river and then turned to me. "Have you ever thought about doing it with a woman?"

"Thought about it! Faye, I wasn't kidding when I told Eunice I was gay before college."

"Molly, you shit! All this time we've been room-mates and you never told me that."

"You never asked."

"People don't think of those things to ask. You are really a hot shit. So besides Frank at Phi Delt you've been going out with girls. I can't believe you, you are too fucking much."

"No, sorry to disappoint you, but I haven't been dating anyone but Frank the fullback."

"Well, I am pissed you didn't tell me. Here we go through my abortion, I tell you everything and you don't tell me this one thing about yourself. Come to think of it, you don't talk about yourself much anyway. What other secrets are you hiding, Mata Hari?"

"Faye, it's not like this big thing that I keep locked up inside. There wasn't any reason to tell you. Besides my mind is occupied with a lot of other things than the fact that I've slept with some girls."

"You're a hot shit. I know you've slept with men but women. I am truly impressed."

"Why don't you shut up so I can go to sleep?"

Faye collapsed on her bed with a huffed noise. I beat my pillow so part of it would be flat. I can't stand overweight pillows.

"Molly."

"What, Goddammit."

"Let's fuck."

"Faye, you crack me up."

"That's my line and I'm serious. Come on."

"No, period."

"Why not?"

"It's a long story. My experiences with non-lesbians who want to sleep with me have been gross."

"How can you be a non-lesbian and sleep with another woman?"

"Beats me, but the last girl I slept with had it all figured out in her twisted brain."

"Now that I'm dying of curiosity and insulted by your refusal you'd better tell me about these non-lesbians before I swallow my tongue and turn purple in the face. If you don't, I'll scream and tell Mother you tried to rape me."

Faye faked a noiseless scream. I immediately told her my tale of woe.

"That was a raw deal. After that, I'd go celibate."

"I did."

"Break it. Come over here and sleep with me. I promise not to be a non-lesbian."

"Your sense of humor overwhelms me."

Faye jumped out of bed, threw the covers off me and declared, "If you won't come over to me I'll come over to you. Now I am Goddamned, fucking serious. Move your ass over." She plopped down next to me, "Now what do I do? I never did this before?"

"Faye, I can see this is going to be the beginning of a beautiful relationship."

"You and Humphrey Bogart. Molly, I do want to make love." She hugged me and gave me a kiss on the forehead. "Okay, so maybe part of it is curiosity but another part of it is that I have more fun with you than anyone else in the whole fucking world. I probably love you more than anybody. This is the way it should be, you know, a lover who is a friend and not that moonie crap." She gave me a long, soft kiss. She was serious. In times like this, intellectual analysis does no damn good so I swept away thoughts of the aftermath and kissed her neck, her shoulders, and returned to her mouth.

The rest of that semester we spent in bed, emerging only to go to class and to eat. Faye made her grades because it was the only way we could be together, and she stopped drinking because she found something that was more fun. Chi Omega began to think Faye had died and gone to heaven. Tri Delta resorted to sending me urgent notices in the mail. We were eighteen, in love, and didn't know the world existed—but it knew we existed.

Not until February did I notice that people on our hall weren't speaking to us anymore. Conversations stopped when one or both of us would amble down the brown halls. Faye concluded they all had chronic laryngitis and decided she'd cure it. She hooked up a Mickey Mouse Club record to the ugly brick bell tower that rang class changes. Then she announced to our dorm neighbors that at three-thirty the true nature of the university would be revealed via the bell tower. As soon as the record blared across the campus Dot and Karen ran in from next door to giggle at Faye's success. Just as quickly they turned on their heels to walk out when Faye bluntly asked, "How come you two don't talk to us anymore?"

Terror crossed Dot's face and she told a half truth. "Because you stay in your room all the time."

"Bullshit," Faye countered.

"There's got to be another reason," I added.

Karen, angered at our bad manners in being so

direct, spat at us gracefully. "You two are together so much it looks like you're lesbians."

I thought Faye was going to heave her chemistry book at Karen, her white face was so red. I looked Karen right in the face and said calmly, "We are."

Karen reeled back as though she were slapped with a soggy dishrag. "You're sick and you don't belong in a place like this with all these girls around."

Faye was now on her feet moving toward Karen, and Dot, the picture of courage, was at the door fumbling with the knob. Faye shifted into overdrive and roared her engine, "Why, Karen, are you afraid I might sleep with you? Are you afraid I might sneak over in the middle of the night and attack you?" Faye was laughing by this time and Karen was petrified. "Karen, if you were the last woman on earth, I'd go back to men—you're a simpering, pimply-faced cretin." Karen ran out the room and Faye howled, "Did you see her face? What an insipid asswipe that creature is!"

"Faye, we're in for it now. She's gonna run right to the resident counselor and we are gonna be in real fucking trouble. They'll probably throw us out."

"Let them. Who the hell wants to rot in this institution of miseducation?"

"I do. It's my one chance to get out of the boondocks. I've got to get my degree."

"We'll go to a private school."

"You can go to a private school. I can't even pay for my own food, Goddammit."

"Look, my old man will pay my way and we can work part time to pay your way. Shit I wish he'd give you the money. I don't give a rat's ass about my degree. But that's out of the question. Anyway, he wants me to stay in school, so he'll send bonuses to encourage me and we can get along with that plus a little work."

"I think it's going to be harder than that, Faye, but I hope you're right."

One half-hour after Faye insulted Karen's non-existent sexuality, she was called to the resident counselor's office while I was sent to the dean of women, Miss Marne. This creature was a heifer-like, red-haired woman who had been a major in the Army Corps back in World War II. She liked to quote her military experiences as proof that women could make it. I walked into her *House & Garden* office with all the painted plaques on the wall. She probably had one up there as proof of her femininity too. She smiled broadly and shook my hand vigorously.

"Sit down, won't you, Miss Bolt? Have a cigarette?"

"No thank you, I don't smoke."

"Wise of you. Now, let's get down to business. I called you here because of the unfortunate incident in your dormitory. Would you care to explain that to me?"

"No."

"Miss Bolt, this is a very serious matter and I want to help you. It will be much easier if you cooperate." She ran her hand over the glass cover on her maplewood desk and smiled reassuringly. "Molly, may I call you that?" I nodded. What the hell do I care what she calls me? "I've been going over your record and you're one of our most outstanding students—an honors scholar, tennis team, freshman representative, Tri-Delta—you're a go-getter, as we say. Ha, ha. I think you're the kind of young woman who will want to work out this problem that you have and I want to help you work it out. A person like you could go far in this world." She lowered her voice confidentially. "I know it's been hard for you, your birth and well, you simply didn't have the advantages of other girls. That's why I admire the way you've risen above your circumstances. Now tell me about this difficulty you have in relating to girls and your roommate."

"Dean Marne, I don't have any problem relating to girls and I'm in love with my roommate. She makes me happy."

Her scraggly red eyebrows with the brown pencil glaring through shot up. "Is this relationship with Faye Raider of an, uh—intimate nature?"

"We fuck, if that's what you're after."

I think her womb collapsed on that one. Sputtering, she pressed forward. "Don't you find that somewhat of an aberration? Doesn't this disturb you, my dear? After all, it's not normal."

"I know it's not normal for people in this world to be happy, and I'm happy."

"H-m-m. Perhaps there are things hidden in your past, secrets in your unconscious that keep you from having a healthy relationship with members of the opposite sex. I think with some hard work on your part and professional assistance, you can uncover these blocks and find the way to a deeper, more meaningful relationship with a man." She took a breath and smiled that administrative smile. "Haven't you ever thought about children, Molly?"

"No."

This time she couldn't hide her shock. "I see. Well dear, I have arranged for you to see one of our psychiatrists here three times a week and of course, you'll see me once a week. I want you to know I'm in there rooting for you to get through this phase you're in. I want you to know I'm your friend."

If I had had a blow torch, I'd have turned it on her smiling face until it was as red as her hair. I didn't have one in my purse, so I did the next best thing. "Dean Marne, why are you pushing me so hard to be a mother and all that rot when you aren't even married?"

She squirmed in her seat and avoided my gaze. I had broken the code and put her on the spot. "We're here to discuss you, not me. I had plenty of opportunities. I decided a career was more important to me than being a homemaker. Many ambitious women were forced into that choice in my day."

"You know what I think? I think you're as much a lesbian as I am. You're a goddamn fucking closet fairy, that's what you are. I know you've been living with Miss Stiles of the English Department for the last fifteen years. You're running this whole number on me to make yourself look good. Hell, at least I'm honest about what I am."

Yes, her face was red, inflamed. She slammed her fist so hard on the desk that the glass covering with all the papers pushed under it broke and she cut her meaty hand. "Young lady, you are going directly to the psychiatrist. You are obviously a hostile, destructive personality and need supervision. What a way to talk to me when I'm trying to help you. You're farther gone than I thought."

The noise attracted her secretaries and Dean Marne dialed the university hospital. I was escorted to the looney ward by two campus policemen. The nurse took my fingerprints. I suppose they run them under a microscope to see if there are any diseased bacteria on them. Then I was led to a bare room with a cot in it and stripped of all my clothing. I was put in a nifty gown that would have made even Marilyn Monroe look whipped. The door was shut and they turned the key. The flourescent lights hurt my eyes and their humming was driving me as nuts as the treatment I had received. Hours later Dr. Demiral, a Turkish psychiatrist, came in to talk to me. He asked me if I was disturbed. I told him that I sure was disturbed now and I wanted out of this place. He told me to calm myself, and within a few days I'd be out. Until that time I was being observed for my own good. It was a matter of procedure, nothing personal. Those next days I beat out Bette Davis for acting awards. I was calm and cheerful. I pretended I was delighted to see Dr. Demiral's greasy, bearded face. We talked about my childhood, about Dean Marne, and about my simmering hatreds that I had repressed. It was very simple. Whatever they say, you look serious, attentive, and say "yes" or, "I hadn't thought of that." I invented horrendous stories to ground my fury in the past. It's also very important to make up dreams. They love dreams. I used to lie awake nights thinking up dreams. It was exhausting.

Within the week, I was released to return to the relative tranquility of Broward Hall.

I stopped at my mailbox, which had two letters in it. One was written in Faye's handwriting and one had a silver, blue, and gold edging around it which meant it was from my beloved sisters at Tri-Delta. I opened that one first. It was official and had the crescent seal on the paper. I was dropped from the sorority and they were sure I'd understand. Everyone hoped I'd get better. I ran up the stairs, opened the door, and found all Faye's things gone. I sat down on the lonesome bed and read Faye's letter.

Dear Sweet Lover Molly,

The resident counselor told me my father is coming to pick me up and I'm to pack everything. Daddy is apparently close to a heart attack over this whole thing because as soon as I got out of my disgusting discussion with the R.C. I called home and Mums answered the phone. She sounded as though she had swallowed a razor blade. She said I'd better have an explanation for all this because Dad's ready to put me in the funny farm to "straighten me out." God, Molly, they're all *crazy*. My own parents want to lock me up. Mother was crying and said she'd get the best doctors there were for her little girl and what did she do wrong. Vomit! I think we won't see each other. They'll keep me away and you're locked up in the hospital. I feel like I'm underwater. I'd run away by myself but I can't seem to move and sounds roll in and out of my head like waves. I think I won't surface until I see you. It looks like I won't see you soon. If they put me away maybe I'll never see you. Molly, get out of here. Get out and don't try to find me. There's no time for us now. Everything is stacked against us. Listen to me. I may be underwater but I can see some things. Get out of here. Run. You're the stronger of the two of us. Go to a big city. It ought to be a little better there. Be free. I love you.

Faye

P.S. $20 is all I had left in my account. It's in your top drawer with all the underpants. I left an old bottle of Jack Daniels there too. Drink a toast to me and then fly away.

Between a white pair of underpants and a red pair was the twenty dollars. Underneath the whole pile was the Jack Daniels. I drank Faye her toast, then walked down the hall with all the doors closing like clockwork and poured the rest of the bottle down the drain.

The next day in my mailbox was a letter from the scholarship committee informing me that my scholarships could not be renewed for "moral reasons" although my academic record was "superb."

Nesting in the back of my closet with the palmetto bugs was my Girls' State suitcase. I pulled it out and filled it, sat on it to close it. I left my books in my room except for my English book, left my term papers and football programs and my last scrap of innocence. I closed the door forever on idealism and the essential goodness of human nature, and I walked to the Greyhound bus station by the same path that I had taken on my arrival.

Mother was sitting in her green stuffed rocking chair when I walked through the door. "You can turn around and walk right out. I know everything that went on up there, the dean of women called me up. You just turn your ass around and get out."

"Mom, you only know what they told you."

"I know you let your ass run away with your head, that's what I know. A queer, I raised a queer, that's what I know. You're lower than them dirty fruit pickers in the groves, you know that?"

"Mom, you don't understand anything. Why don't you let me tell my side of it?"

"I don't want to hear nothing you can say. You always were a bad one. You never obeyed nobody's rules—mine, the school's, and now you go defying God's rules. Go on and get outa here. I don't want you. Why the hell you even bother to come back here?"

"Because you're the only family I got. Where else am I gonna go?"

"That's your problem, smart-pants. You'll have no friends and you got no family. Let's see how far you get, you little snot-nose. You thought you'd go to college and be better than me. You thought you'd go mix with the rich. And you still think you're dandy, don't you? Even being a stinking queer don't shake you none. I can see conceit writ all over your face. Well, I hope I live to see the day you put your tail between your legs. I'll laugh right in your face."

"Then you'd better live to see me dead." I picked up my suitcase by the door and walked out into the cool night air. I had $14.61 in my jeans, that's what was left over from Faye's money and the remains of mine after the bus ticket. That wouldn't get me half to New York City. And that's where I was going. There are so many queers in New York that one more wouldn't rock the boat.

I walked down northeast 14th Street to Route 1 and there I parked my suitcase on the ground and stuck out my thumb. Nobody seemed to notice me. I was beginning to think I'd have to walk to New York when a station wagon with Georgia plates pulled up.

A man, woman, and child sat inside looking me over. The woman motioned for me to hop in. She started right up. "My husband thought you must be some stranded college student. Came on down here for a break and your money run out, did it?"

"Yes ma'am, that's exactly what happened and you know I couldn't tell my parents I was down here. They'd have fits."

The man chuckled. "Kids. Where do you go to school?"

"Oh, I go to Barnard up in New York City."

"Oh, you do have a long way to go," the woman said.

"Yes ma'am. And I bet you all aren't going up that far are you?"

"No, but we're going as far north as Statesboro, Georgia." She laughed.

"You got spunk hitching," her husband admired. "I've never seen a girl hitch before."

"Maybe you've never seen a girl broke before."

They both roared and agreed that the days of flaming youth were back in style. They were nice people, homey, suburban, and boring, but nice all the same. They warned me not to get in a car with more than one man in it and to try to hold out for a car with a woman passenger. When they left me off at the Gulf station in Statesboro the man gave me a ten-dollar bill and wished me luck. They waved goodbye as they drove off into the sunset of the nuclear family.

I took up under an aging tree drenched in Spanish moss. After three or more hours a car finally pulled over. The driver was near my age, clean-cut, and alone. Well, if he tries anything, I have a fighting chance.

"Hi, how far are you going?"

"All the way to New York City."

"Come on in, you hit the jackpot. I'm going to Boston."

I slung myself into the low Corvette and prayed he wasn't recently released from a mental institution. Maybe he should be praying: I was the one just out of protective custody.

"My name is Ralph. What's yours?"

"Molly Bolt."

"Hi, Molly."

"Hi, Ralph."

"How come you're hitching? That's dangerous, you know that?"

"Yeah, I know that, but I didn't exactly have a fat choice." I launched into my rap about running out of money. Ralph was short, muscular, and had blond, curly hair. He went to M.I.T. and majored in nuclear physics. He was a friendly young man, interested in me, but too polite to lunge. I had latched onto a lucky ride. All I had to do was talk, keep him entertained, and take a turn at the wheel. He was in a hurry to get back so we skipped a potentially gruesome motel scene. The glove compartment was crammed with dex so there was no danger of flaking out. We talked nonstop all the way up the Eastern seaboard. Finally I understood the quantum theory and Ralph understood the rise of Joseph Stalin. At last, when we came through the Holland Tunnel, I understood that there never was a city like New York. I was coming into a foreign land without one friend and very little money.

"Molly, let me drive you to your door. I don't mind at all."

"Thanks, but I'd like to walk around a little. Sounds corny but I really want to do it. Why don't you leave me in Washington Square?" I had read somewhere in some trashy book that the Square was the hub of the Village and the Village was the hub of homosexuality. Ralph dropped me right in front of the arch. He gave me his address, a kiss, and a cheery good-bye and drove off in a puff of carbon gas. I had to fight back an urge to call him back and tell him I didn't know one damn thing about this monstrous city and why not switch schools to New York and be my friend.

The temperature was in the thirties and all I had was a thin jacket with a crew neck sweater on underneath plus $24.61 in my pocket. The Square was not teeming with flashy gay people as I had hoped. I started up Fifth Avenue and tried not to cry. Faces were coming at me in all directions and I didn't know one of them. People were pushing and hurrying and no one smiled, not even a little grin. This wasn't a city, it was some branch of hell, the Hanging Gardens of Neon burning into my skull. Hell or not, there was no place for me to go so this would be my place.

I got as far as 14th Street. The mad shoppers rushing for Mays and Kleins nearly trampled me. I turned around to go back to the Square, at least it was quieter there. It was getting late and an acid drizzle was coming down. Already I could feel the pollution caking in my nostrils and my eyes burning from the fumes. Hunger hit like a semi since the dex wore off, but I was afraid to spend any money on food. I knew I couldn't spend any on a room either. It looked as though I was going to curl up in the fountain in the park and freeze to death. My hands had begun to crack and bleed from carrying my suitcase in the cold. My toes were ice cubes. I didn't have any socks. Who wears socks in Florida? The Square was deserted save for a few couples strolling through and a drunk down by the chess tables. Now what the flying hell am I going to do?

I turned toward New York University and studied the buildings, dimly perceiving they were some type of institution. Maybe I can sneak in there and sleep. I went to the main entrance but it was locked. Then I trotted around to a side entrance on University Place. That door was locked too. Well, I could run around the block all night to keep warm. As I turned, I noticed a wrecked Hudson car. Faded red and black, crumpled up in front with all the tires robbed from its wheels, it slumped in front of the Chock Full O' Nuts. It looked beautiful to me and it was home.

I went over to crawl in the back seat only to find it was occupied but the front seat was empty and the steering wheel was busted so it wouldn't get in the way. I opened the door and slid in. The young man in the back seat lifted his hat off his head with a flourish. "Good evening, Madam. Are you going to share these accommodations with me?"

"If it's okay with you I am."

"It's okay with me." He tipped his hat back over his eyes, pulled his heavy coat over his shoulders, and fell asleep.

The next morning I woke up with him leaning over the front seat poking me. "Hey babe, come on. We gotta get out of here. Time to hustle." I sat up and looked at him in the light. He had the longest eyelashes I had ever seen on anyone. His skin was the color of coffee after you put the cream in and his eyes were clear, deep brown. He had a bristling happy moustache over a full, red mouth. In short, this guy was gorgeous. I was trying to remember where I was and trying to find out if my limbs had dropped off from frostbite.

"Come on. Grab your suitcase and let's go to Chock Full. There's a sister in there who will feed us for free. Up!"

Knots of sleepy students were rushing to make their nine-o'clock class. The revolving door to Chock Full was spinning like a top, and I was so tired I went around twice before I could get myself out. We sat at a counter toward the back and a waitress in a blue uniform served us coffee and donuts. She wrote out a make-believe slip and winked at my roommate. "Got yourself a new girlfriend, Calvin?"

"Not me, I don't go in for girlfriends." He winked back at her.

I looked at him with grateful eyes. "You gay?"

"Oh, I wouldn't say I was gay. I'd just say I was enchanted."

"Me too."

He breathed a sigh of relief and smiled. "Right on. I was afraid you'd be some straight chick up here for an abortion, something like that. Then I'd have to take care of you."

"Why, do you usually take care of the results of unchecked heterosexuality?"

"Every now and then."

"You're not doing such a good job of taking care of yourself if you're sleeping in that car."

"Saves rent. Actually you were lucky to find me at home last night. I usually sleep at the house of whoever I go home with. You get breakfast that way too. But you'd better not plan on that.

Lesbians don't pick each other up on the street. I know a couple bars we can try out tonight and maybe you'll get lucky. You shouldn't have trouble, you're good looking and young, two priceless attributes."

"If it's all the same to you, I think I'll pass that by."

"Oh, I know. You only do it for love."

"Uh—well."

"Do you want to keep sleeping in that car and freeze your ass?"

"No."

"Then you'd better hustle a little, sweetheart." He gave me a pinch on the elbow.

The rest of that day Calvin showed me the subway systems, how the city was laid out, and how to steal food from supermarkets, delicatessens, and even hot dog vendors on the street. We walked all through the Village and he introduced me to the street people—well-dressed numbers runners, hookers, and a few pushers here and there. I liked them. They were the only people who smiled at me.

"Molly, you got any money?"

"$24.61."

"If you aren't gonna hook, babe, you aren't getting no apartment on that dustpile. Now I happen to know how you can make a simple $100 in a half hour and you don't have to fuck or even take your clothes off. Can you dig that?"

"Tell me the deal first."

"There's this guy, Ronnie Rapaport, the grapefruit freak. This cat gets his kicks out of being blasted with grapefruits."

"Come on, Calvin."

"No shit, that's how he does his thing. All you gotta do is go up to his apartment and throw grapefruits at him and he'll pay you $100 in cash. See, part of his thing is he has to have a new person do it every time. Too bad because I'd be up there every night throwing yellow curves at him."

"How can he afford it?"

"They say his old man owns a big department store somewhere out in Queens. Who knows. You ready?"

"Ready-o."

"Did your cheerleaders do that too?"

"I think everybody's does."

"Were you a cheerleader?"

"Nah. I just dated one."

"Oh wow, I used to date a football player."

"Well, we're just All-American queers."

Calvin laughed and danced his way over to a red phone booth filled with the day's collection of papers, cigarette butts, and fresh urine. He called Ronnie and the deal was set. Tonight was fine with him.

"Old Ronnie was practically coming over the phone when I told him you were 18, sweet, and all that good shit."

"Great, maybe he'll give me a bonus for my age."

"Too bad he's a man, too bad for you I mean. Maybe if it were a woman you'd get a little buzz off it, you know what I mean."

"I don't think Greta Garbo'd give me a buzz if I had to pelt her with citrus."

Ronnie had a huge duplex on Hudson. Skylights covered the ceiling and the furniture was stainless-steel-chrome expensive. By looking at him, you couldn't tell he was into grapefruit. He didn't wear any fruit symbols around his neck or have embroidered seeds on his shirt. He shook my hand and took me into the next room. Calvin waited in the big living room and ate pears. I entered another huge room that looked like a photographer's studio, except that it was completely bare except for an enormous pile of grapefruit piled on top of one another like cannon balls. Ronnie took his clothes off. He was well muscled with a patch of curling hair between his breasts. He walked over to the end of the room and stood there quivering. I waited for Carmen Miranda to burst through the door in a giant banana hat. Seeing my hesitation, he said in a gentle voice, "Okay honey, I'm ready." So I picked up a grapefruit and threw it at him. Shit, I missed. It splattered against the wall. This is going to be harder than I thought. I picked up another one and carefully took aim. Squish! I got him square in the middle. He squealed with delight and got a hard on. This isn't so bad. I like throwing things. By now I was into hitting Ronnie. I aimed for his cock. Bulls-eye. He loved it. I aimed for his left shoulder. Only grazed him. I started firing grapefruits like Stonewall Jackson's artillery at Manassas. Blam, blat, splat. Ronnie howled like a wounded dog and I threw the grapefruits even harder, concentrating on his thighs and pulp covered prick. I was down to the last round of grapeshot and began to worry that maybe I'd need more to finish him off. Ronnie knew himself very well because as I picked up one of the remaining four grapefruit he came in an arc of sticky liquid and collapsed on the floor, a lump of spent pleasure. I felt as though I had single-handedly won the Battle of the Bulge. I went over to pick him up. "Molly, you have a wonderful arm." Covered in pink and white pulp he whispered of the delights of my accuracy. Too bad I don't like grapefruit or I would have licked it off of him I was so hungry.

"You okay, Ronnie?"

"Fabulous. I'm simply fabulous."

"Uh, I'm glad to hear that. If you don't need me further I think I'll roll on."

"Oh, of course. Let me give you the money. It was worth every penny. Last person I had with an arm like that throws for the Mets." He got up and walked into the next room where Calvin had wiped out the entire bowl of pears. Ronnie handed me five twenty-dollar bills, new. "Calvin, thank you for bringing me this love. She was too, too perfect. Come back sometime, Molly. I can't do it twice with the same person but come back and talk to me. You look like a nice kid."

When we hit the street, the cold seemed twice as bad probably because I was so hungry. "You ate all the fruit, pig. I'm starving. Where can we go eat where they won't take all my hard-earned cash?"

"I know where we can eat for free. Come on."

We went to The Finale. Turns out Calvin used to have a thing there with the waiter so he slipped us steak. My stomach had shrunk so much that I couldn't eat but half of it. We put the rest in a doggy bag and returned to the cold.

"I'm not ready to go back to the car and freeze. Let's go to that bar you were telling me about?"

We went over to Eighth Avenue and turned in at a quiet-looking place with a black-and-white-striped awning. Inside, the room was packed with women and a straight john here and there. We pushed our way to the bar.

"Two Harvey Wallbangers," Calvin yelled. "Is it okay if we spend some of your loot?"

"Sure. You got me the job, so you ought to have part of it."

"No thanks. All I want is a drink or two, then I have to go out and hustle for a place to stay tonight. Too damn cold in that car. First let's see if we can get you set up. Who knows, maybe some lady will be kind and put you up without having you put out. Oh, here comes a bull and she's heading straight for you. Christ, go to bed with her and she'll crush you."

Sure enough this diesel dyke barrels down on me, slams on her brakes, and bellows, "Hi there. My name is Mighty Mo. You must be new around here. I've never seen your face before."

"Yes ma'am. I'm new." God, the Mo must stand for Moron.

"Ma'am? Why honey, you all must be from down South. Ha. Ha."

If she weren't so damn big I'd belt her one right now. Yankees are compelled by some mysterious force to imitate Southern accents and they're so damn dumb they don't know the difference between a Tennessee drawl and a Charleston clip. "Yes, I'm from Florida."

"You must be crazy. Why did you ever leave that sunshine to come up here to this cold witch's tit?" More laughter.

"Guess I like cold witch's tits."

She thought that was a witty reply and nearly knocked me over with a bellylaugh. "That's a good one. Speaking of tits, sugar, are you butch or femme?"

I looked at Calvin but there wasn't time for him to give me a clue for this one. "I beg your pardon?"

"Now don't be coy with Mighty Mo, you Southern belle. They have butches and femmes down below the Mason-Dixon line, don't they? You're a looker baby and I'd like to get to know you, but if you're butch then it'd be like holding hands with your brother now wouldn't it?"

"Your tough luck, Mo. Sorry." Sorry my ass. Thank God she spilled the beans.

"You sure fooled me. I thought you were femme. What's this world coming to when you can't tell the butches from the femmes. Ha. Ha." She slapped me on the back fraternally and sauntered off.

"What the flying fuck is this?"

"A lot of these chicks divide up into butch and femme, male-female. Some people don't, but this bar is into heavy roles and it's the only bar I know for women. I thought you knew about that stuff or I wouldn't have sprung it on you."

"That's the craziest, dumbass thing I ever heard tell of. What's the point of being a lesbian if a woman is going to look and act like an imitation man? Hell, if I want a man, I'll get the real thing not one of these chippies. I mean, Calvin, the whole point of being gay is because you love women. You don't like men that look like women, do you?"

"Oh, me, I'm not picky as long as he has a big cock. I'm a bit of a size queen."

"Goddammit. I'm not either one. Now what the fuck do I do?"

"Since you're here, you'd better choose sides for a warm bed."

"Shit."

"Ah, come on, it's not that bad for one night."

"It seems to me that if I say I'm femme then the Mighty Moes of the world will descend upon me, but if I say I'm butch then I have to pay for the drinks. Either way I get screwed."

"The human condition."

"Oh no, here comes another one. Well she looks like a woman so that's a point in her favor. She also looks like a good forty if she's a day and totally wasted. Damn, son of a bitch, hell—I can't hack this. Come on, Calvin, let's split."

Back on the street again, I felt myself getting used to the city. "Look, I'm going back to the car. You go on and pick up a trick. Don't worry about me. It's too cold for rapists to be roaming the streets. Anyway at least they won't ask me if I am butch or femme."

"Nah, I don't feel much like hustling anyway. I think I got the clap. Let's go on back to the car."

"Tomorrow morning I'll find an apartment and we can both live there. No more cars. Okay?"

That night it was so cold I took the few clothes out of my suitcase and covered Calvin and myself with them but it didn't work very well. We finally gave up on sleep and huddled together in the back seat waiting for the sun to come up and Chock Full to open so we could warm our guts on hot coffee.

"Calvin, how come you're here out on the street?"

"How come you're here out on the street?"

"You first."

"There's not a lot to tell. I used to live in Philly. We had a fair-sized family, me, my brother, and one sister. I'm the middle one. My older brother was a big jock and I didn't follow in his footsteps. I acted in all the class plays at school and thought that's what I wanted to do. That didn't sit well with my family. Then the kids at school started giving me the business about being a fairy, called me the African Queen. Shit, every stud in that school was sucked off at one time or another, but I got caught at it. It was a big, Goddamn mess. My momma starts calling out to Jesus and my old man tells me he's gonna bust my head. I cried and allowed as how I'd change and go straight and all that shit. Damn, didn't I get this girl pregnant. Well, that's what they wanted, wasn't it? It didn't change anything for me. I still wanted men. She's a nice girl and all that. I could have lived with her and had kids, if I could have kept seeing men. But you know how that is. People are so dumb. You fuck a little with a member of the opposite sex and you got your straight credentials in order. Hell! Well, Mom and Dad were after me now to marry this girl. I ain't marrying no girl. So I ran away and here I am. I been here for about a month. I do think about that girl, her name's Pat,

but I ain't going back there and marrying her."
He paused for a minute then asked me, "Do you
think I'm a shit for leaving her?"

"It does sort of leave her up shit creek without
a paddle, Calvin. She's the one stuck with the kid;
you take off scot free."

"Yeah, I know. But if I go back there and marry
her then I have to get a job and have my brains
ground out like everybody else. My old man is a
schoolteacher. He thinks he's really something
because he's better than some janitor, you know.
But he ain't so hot. He goes to work like everyone
else and when he walks on the street he's a nigger
like anyone else. He's blind in one eye and can't
see out the other. I'm not about to do that
number."

"When all this happened did you talk to Pat
about an abortion?"

"Sure I did. She screamed and carried on about
how that was murder and here was the fruit of
our love. I nearly threw up on that one. Girl's got
no sense. She thinks motherhood's gonna make
her a natural woman or something. Wait until
that little beast starts crying in the middle of the
night. She'll wish she'd listened to me. She was
determined that I'd marry her and settle down
and we'd have a picture book family and get
photographed for *Ebony* someday. Shit."

"Then I guess she'll learn the hard way. I'm glad
you tried to change her mind, but maybe that's all
she's got. You know how some girls are. They think
they're nothing until they get married and have a
baby. So now she's getting her baby, although she's
minus the marriage bit."

"Why are you here? You haven't told me your story."

I recounted my tales of horror.

"Damn, they get you coming and they get you going, don't they? Looks like nobody wants their queers, not the whites, not the blacks. I bet even the Chinese don't want their queers."

"I don't much care what any of them want, Calvin. I just care about what I want, the hell with all of them."

"Yeah, that's what I think too."

"Hey, the sun's coming up. I hope Chock Full opens early today. Don't forget, I'm looking for an apartment today. You want to come?"

"You know what I'm going to do today? I'm going out there on the turnpike and hitch to California. I mean it. If you could hitch up here from Florida I can hitch out to San Francisco. Come on with me?"

"I would. This is going to sound weird, Calvin, but something tells me I have to stay in this ugly city for awhile. I don't know how long, but I have to be here. It's like I'll make my fortune here or something. Remember those old children's stories where the young son goes out on the road for adventure and to make his fortune after he's been cheated out of his inheritance by his evil brothers?"

"Yeah, I sort of remember those. Puss-in-Boots kind of thing?"

"Yeah, kinda like that."

"Well, I'm going to San Francisco for mine."

Finally Chock Full opened and our waitress supplied us with goodies. We both took a long time

dunking our donuts because neither one of us
wanted to start out on that day. But we had to pry
ourselves off the thinly padded stools. On the
street, we looked at each other, then slowly
stretched out our right hands. It was a very formal
handshake, almost like a ritual. Then we wished
each other luck and went off in opposite directions
to seek our fortunes.

Near the river on West 17th Street, I found a ragged apartment. The bathtub was in the kitchen, the electricity was d.c., and the walls were layers of multicolor from so many coats of paint and wallpaper peeling over decades of misuse. Rent was $62.50 a month. My first piece of furniture was a used single-bed mattress someone had graciously left on the street. I drug it back up five flights of stairs and beat it until I thought it was clean enough to touch.

The next day I got a job at The Flick serving ice cream and hamburgers in a bunnyesque costume. I made enough to cover rent plus I filched as much food as I could from the ptomaine pits at work. After the subway and incidentals I had about $5.00 a week for myself. That sum I hoarded until the weekend when I'd go to the bars, where secretaries from New Jersey met secretaries from the Bronx and they lived happily ever after. Standing next to the wrought-iron railing at Sugar's bar with its New Orleans whorehouse red decor I would swear to myself that I wasn't coming back next weekend. I couldn't hack the games and I felt like a complete fool going over to some woman and asking her to dance. And the ones who came over to ask me to dance left their Mack trucks parked outside. Boredom set in my bones but I didn't know where else to turn. So every weekend I broke the vow I made the weekend before, and I came back to lean against the wrought iron railing and look at the ladies.

One Friday night I was spared the red velvet womb of Sugar's. A young woman showed up at The Flick and ordered chocolate chip ice cream and expresso. She looked straight into my eyes and said, "With a body like that you ought to try something different from waiting on tables."

"Who me?" I nearly dropped the ice cream in her crotch.

"You. When do you get off work?"

"Twelve."

"I'm coming back here to pick you up at twelve."

Jesus H. Christ on a raft. I've just been picked up by a spectacular, six-foot woman. Hot damn, New York may turn out to be something good after all.

Twelve o'clock and she was there in a long black cape with a Napoleon collar. It made her look even taller and the high collar drew attention to a perfect nose underneath arching brows. Her name was Holly. She was 25, born in Illinois with no apparent ambition other than to attract attention. She asked me if there were any job openings at The Flick. There were, and the next day Holly was hired by Larry the Leech who slobbered when he caught sight of her 34C in a leotard. Holly and I worked the same hours and the same area. She must have spent half her wages on me but money didn't seem to matter to her. It was fine with me if she spent her money on me, if she didn't care. We went to see every show in the city on our nights off and when there wasn't anything we wanted to see she'd take me to my door, kiss me goodbye, and swoop off in her black cape. I was having a hard time figuring her out.

Maybe I need to doctor myself up a little. With that in mind I went out in the early morn haze with my pea coat on and less than a dollar in my pocket. Two hours later I returned with a bottle of Madam Rochas, a can of shaving cream, a copy of *The New York Review of Books, Variety*, three Reese's peanut butter cups, one steak, one package of frozen spinach that had turned my shirt green and froze my liver, razor blades, eye shadow, mascara and a felt tip pen. That night when I went to work I had on the eye shadow, mascara and Madam Rochas, but Holly didn't notice or maybe she thought I was fine without warpaint.

We got off at twelve and she took me to a new bar on 72nd Street called the Penthouse. You had to have an expensive membership card to get in but Holly produced one.

"Holly, how did you get the money for that?"

"I didn't. An actress gave it to me."

"Out of the goodness of her heart?"

"Partially. She's my lover."

"Oh."

"I'm a kept woman, if that's what you're thinking."

"I wasn't thinking anything at all, but I'd have hit on that eventually."

"Now that you know my terrible secret," her voice quivered in mock terror, "are you going to walk out of my life forever?"

"No, but if you have money and all that, why the hell do you work at the salt mines?"

"Keeps me grounded in reality."

"Who wants that kind of reality? I've been in it all my life. I'd like another brand."

"Well, I like it for awhile. It's a trip, you know."

"Yeah. Say, who is this actress lady?"

"Would you believe me if I told you Marie Dressler?"

"She's dead, smartass, but she happens to be my all time, favorite actress. Come on, tell."

"Kim Wilson."

"No shit?"

"No shit."

"How did you meet her?"

"That's a long story. I don't feel like getting into it. Anyway, she's okay even if she's over forty. If you want to meet her there's going to be a big party at Chryssa Hart's—you know, the archeologist. I'll be with Kim, but we can all go together as long as I go home with her. Just wait until Chrys lowers her blue eyes on you. That ought to be rich."

"Spare me the details. She's seventy years old, had her face lifted five times, and drips diamonds wherever she walks."

"She does drip diamonds, but she's forty something and very, uh, well preserved."

"Great, what does she do, sleep in an alcohol bath? I get pursued by the human pickle. Some friend you are, fixing me up with the geriatric ward."

"I'm trying to help you out of your crushing poverty, love. I don't feel like talking about middle-aged ladies. Let's dance."

We passed through a long bar, then a crowded room with a stone fireplace, another room, and finally arrived at the enormous square floor with the ubiquitous mirror ball glittering from the ceiling. For all its splash and Broadway clientele, it was a friendly place. Other women and men talked to us, bought us drinks and invited us to parties. Neither of us noticed what time it was until we caught sight of the sky lightening outside the window.

"Look, it is beautiful sometimes, this city. Must be four a.m. and I'm not even tired," I said.

"Me neither. I only live a few blocks from here. Why don't we go to my place?"

Ah ha. Finally.

Holly lived on West End Avenue in a big apartment with lots of old molding on the ceilings and parquet floors. A monstrous silver Persian, Gertrude Stein, greeted us at the door and she was pissed that Holly stayed out so late. On our journey through the apartment we found a trail of feline discontent: a chewed slipper, a shredded corner of the rug, and when we passed the bathroom we saw that Gertrude Stein had pulled the entire roll of toilet paper off the roller.

"Is she always this vindictive?"

"Yes, but then I look forward to her little surprises. You know, of course, that we are heading toward the bedroom and that we're going in there to make love?"

"I know."

"Then why are you walking so slow? Come on, run." Holly trotted into a bedroom boasting an enormous brass bed with a plush maroon bedspread. Halfway to the bed she had her blouse off. "Hurry up."

"I'm going slow so as not to arouse Gertrude's suspicion in case she's the jealous type." Sure enough, Gertrude was paddling after me with hostility in her slanted eyes.

"You're safe. Gerty will only try to slither between us."

"Wonderful. I've never done it with a cat before." Holly had all her clothes off and was rolling down the bedspread. She was more beautiful out of her clothes than in them. I tripped getting out of my pants.

"Molly, you really should dance. You're all sinew and muscle and you look terrific. Come here."

She pulled me on the bed and I was close to passing out from being next to six feet of smooth flesh. She was running her fingers through my hair, biting my neck, and I started floating on hot energy. She had a soft, thick afro which she slid all over my body. And she kept biting me. Her tongue ran along the back of my ear, into my ear, down my neck, along my shoulder bone and on down to my breasts, then back up to my mouth. I lost track of linear sequence after that, but I know she put the full weight of her body on top of mine and I thought I was going to scream she felt so fine. I ran my hands down her back and could barely reach her behind she was so long. Each time she moved I could feel the muscles under her skin fluidly changing shape. The woman was a demon. She started slow and got wilder and wilder until she was holding me so tight I couldn't breathe and I didn't care. I could feel her inside me, outside me, all over me; I didn't know where her body began and mine left off. One of us was yelling but I don't know who it was or what she was yelling. Hours later we untangled ourselves to notice that the sun was high over the Hudson, snow was falling in the river, and Gertrude had devoured my right shoe, my only pair.

"Molly, do you ever make it with men?"

"Why do you ask that?"

"I don't know. I guess after making love like that I hate to think of you wasting it on a man."

"Well, I do it sometimes but not very often. Once you know what women are like, men get kind of boring. I'm not trying to put them down, I mean I like them sometimes as people, but sexually they're dull. I suppose if a woman doesn't know any better, she thinks it's good stuff."

"Yeah, I'll never forget when I found out the difference."

"How old were you?"

"Twenty-two. I'd been sleeping with guys since I was eighteen but it took me four more years to get to women. I think I had spent those twenty-two years ignoring women. I blocked out anything sexual until one night my roommate unblocked me. We were doing summer stock, *Anything Goes* for the wrinkle set, and my roommate was one of the angels. She threw me in bed, really. I kicked and took a chunk out of her arm but that didn't last long. She wouldn't let go and I didn't want her to, secretly. Then I spent the next three weeks running away from her and telling her I didn't like it at all and I only gave in because I was tired of fighting. Guess I fucked her over. If I knew where she was, I'd thank her for throwing me in that bed. She knew, and I didn't."

"So what happened?"

"The show ended and I came back here for auditions. She went out West and like a stupid ass I didn't sleep with her on our last night. I was still busy being a professional heterosexual. Every time I think about that, my stomach turns over."

"I'm certainly grateful to that lady, wherever she is. Here I am reaping the benefits of her courage."

"Opportunist." And she wrapped her arms around me for an instant replay.

Saturday I met Holly at her apartment. Kim was there in a deep red outfit with a black and white scarf. She looked pretty much like she did in the movies except for the false eyelashes, plus she loaded her face with makeup to hide the wrinkles and put on her lipstick with a palette knife, to hide her shrinking lipline, I guess. Other than those attempts at youth, she was good look- ing. I was fully expecting her to sit there with a drink in her hand and bore me with tales of being on the set with Rock Hudson and wasn't it funny when Jack Lemmon fell out of the boat before the cameras started rolling, ha, ha . . . a million laughs from a faded Hollywood that my generation doesn't give a shit about. Instead she talked about Lévi-Strauss and structuralism and how she was getting into Susan Sontag's work. But she wasn't pretentious about it. She seemed to care for Holly a great deal—her eyes followed wherever Holly moved. Gertrude the glutton was napping in her lap and staring out at me from the one green eye she held open for spying purposes.

"Do you like cats?" she asked me.

"I love cats, but I'm not sure about Gerty Gerty Stein Stein. Underneath that silver breast beats the heart of an incurable sadist."

"She is revengeful. She reminds me of a cat we had when I was a child."

You were a child? Right, I guess we all were once upon a time. "Where did you grow up?"

"In the slums of Chicago."

"No shit! I mean, you did?" Kim laughed at me and said yes she did. "Well, I grew up on a dirt farm and picked potato bugs."

"And here we are."

Holly turned. "Oh, super, two bosom members of the proletariat. Spare me tales of how poverty is good for your character."

The color ran to my face but Kim saved me from firing back. "Well, if we're bosom members of the proletariat then I'll take advantage of it." She leaned over and kissed me on the cheek. Holly laughed and the tension evaporated.

I liked Kim a lot. I wished she'd take all that

glop off her face. Why do women do that? She had good bones and that's what counts.

"We ought to get over to Chryssa's soon. Are you two ready?"

Kim and I picked up our coats, and I was embarrassed by my pea coat. She didn't notice or was above noticing.

The town house was in the East Sixties and when we arrived a butler actually took our coats. That was good; kept my ratty blue coat out of the way and the hostess didn't get to see it.

Holly swept into the room grandly and Kim and I followed like attendants. A slender, sun-tanned woman with page-boy hair came over and gave Holly, then Kim a kiss. "Kim, darling, so glad you could come."

"I wouldn't miss one of your parties for the world, Chrys. I'd like you to meet Molly Bolt, a friend of Holly's and a new friend of mine."

Chrys looked at me with as much subtlety as a vulture. She took my hand in both of hers and intoned, "I'm delighted to have you. Come right over here and tell me what you want to drink and then we can chat like civilized human beings." There were over fifty women in the room and as Chrys paraded me across the floor, a slight smirk visited their faces. "What will you have?"

"A Harvey Wallbanger."

"Marvelous. Louis, fix this divine creature a Harvey Wallbanger, with the emphasis on the bang. Now tell me what you do and all those things that one opens a conversation with. Then I'll tell you what I do and we can move from there." Slight laugh.

"At this moment I happen to be a waitress."

"How colorful. But that's not what you really want to do, of course."

"No, I want to go to film school."

"How interesting. Do you want to act or something like that?"

"No, I want to direct but I may have to change my sex in order to get a job."

"Don't do that." She put her arm around my shoulder and whispered in my ear, "We'll see what we can do about breaking the sex barrier in film."

Pause. Then I asked, "You're an archeologist?"

"Yes, but I'll bet you don't want to hear about me digging and dashing about in those dirty trenches, do you?"

"Not at all. In fact, I was reading the other day about N.Y.U.'s dig at Aphrodisios."

Her eyebrows went up, a note of sarcasm crept into her voice. "Yes, but they're botching the job. Now, on my dig, we are uncovering fabulous things, simply fabulous. Last summer I discovered the breast of Artemis done by one of the pupils of Phidias. I'm sure of it."

"I read about it in the *Post*."

She totally brightened, "Oh, they tried to stir up controversy about it, of course. Those parasites will do anything for copy."

A square woman in a tweedy suit lumbered over and bellowed, "Chrys, are you boring this young thing with tales of broken pots and torn fingernails? Really, dear, I'll never understand how you can get excited about all that dirt and shattered housewares."

"You're a cultural infidel, Fritza. This is Molly Bolt, aspiring film director, an American Mai Zetterling."

Fritza smiled, "We need one. I'm sick to death of John Ford."

Chrys flashed a rapier grin at the woman. "Fritza is a true philistine. She's a stockbroker—the ultimate in tedium but it has made her disgustingly rich."

"Yes, and Chrys relieves me of a sizable portion to help finance her dig."

"It's your cultural dues, darling."

"I tend to think of it as alimony, myself."

"Fritza, you're a cad." Chrys linked her arm in mine. "Now, I'm freeing this delicious woman from the clutches of your heavyhanded humor." We started through the crowd leaving Fritza to her drink. "Pay no attention to Fritza. She was my first lover at Bryn Mawr and we've grown comfortable in our hostility."

"Chryssa, Iris is here," a voice called from the crowd.

"Excuse me, Molly, I'll be back as soon as I can."

Holly and Kim came over to me and Holly snickered, "See, I told you she'd flip out over you. She likes dark-haired women with strong faces. I bet her ovaries hit the floor when you walked through the door."

"My irresistible charm, ladies." I lifted my glass for a toast: "to ovaries."

"To ovaries," they echoed. Then Holly scampered off in the direction of a waving arm with too many gold bracelets on it.

"What do you think of the party?" Kim asked.

"I don't know. I haven't had time to talk to anyone except Chrys and her friend, Fritza."

"The gruesome twosome. That's been going on since 1948 when they graduated from Bryn Mawr."

"She mentioned Bryn Mawr but not the year."

"Naturally."

"Want to go over there on that bench and sit down for a bit?"

"Sure."

"I promise not to ask you any questions about your career."

"Good. I'm running away from it. I can't act anyway. Do you mind if I ask you a personal question?"

"No, I don't think I believe in those kind of separations anyway."

"That I'll keep in mind. Are you sleeping with Holly?"

"Yes."

"I thought so. You know she took that job at The Flick so she could get to know you. She told me about it. She's very honest."

"Does it bother you?"

"No, not really. Once I got beyond thirty-five I stopped being torn up about those things and I definitely gave up on monogamy. Maybe I can do it but no one else seems to be able to."

"Well, don't test yourself. Non-monogamy makes life much more interesting."

Kim laughed and looked at me. Her eyes were very light blue-gray. There was something good about her that radiated through her eyes. "That's another thing you've said that I'll keep in mind. Here comes another question—got your fielder's glove on?"

"Check."

"Do you love Holly?"

"No. I like her a lot. In time I think I could love her too, but I don't think I'll ever be in love with her. We're too different."

"How?"

"Oh, Holly's impressed with names and money. She doesn't have much ambition, I think. I do. I don't care about who's got what. I care about getting to school and getting on with my work. She doesn't understand that but as long as we go out for fun there isn't any friction."

"Well look here in the corner: beauty and the beast. Aha!" Chryssa popped her head over a lethargic palm. "Really, Kim, you keep all the young ones to yourself. If you were a man, they'd call you a chicken queen."

From the greatly increased crowd a voice called out, "Chryssa!"

"It's simply impossible to talk at my own party. Molly, have lunch with me next Thursday at one —Four Seasons."

"One, next Thursday," I replied. She gave my hand a squeeze and disappeared back into the mass.

"Better wear your chastity belt."

"Haven't got one. Do you think B.O. will do the trick?"

Lunch with Chryssa was an exercise in evasion. Since I had borrowed all the clothes on my back I was afraid to lift a fork to my mouth. Suppose something would slip off into my right tit and I'd wreck the damn blouse? And the questions from Chryssa—sly and charming but all leading to the same conclusion. I strained to be pleasant and kill the last gasp of a Southern accent. But I nearly lost my restraint when she hinted she'd pay my way through film school, if only. Somehow I got through it without slopping whipped cream on myself and without committing myself.

Riding the subway home I watched the people watching me. I had on nice clothes so I was getting stares of idle curiosity, and even approval, rather than the usual bitter searching eye. Didn't Florence always say that clothes make the man? Oh, for sure, Florence. What the hell were they doing now that I was riding the BMT? Right this minute? If they could see me they'd think I was rich. The hell with them. Why am I thinking about them anyway? Why did that woman in her well-modulated voice try to buy me off? I know why, I know good and why. Shit, what do I do now? I can't run a kept number. I know it's fucked not to be able to do it. Hell, I should take her money and go to school. Her old man got rich off the backs of the poor anyway. Part of the money is my inheritance. Retribution. I should take the Goddamned stuff. How can I pay for school myself? A semester is $1,000. Goddamn being poor. I got to use my ass to save my head. Well, fuck you, Chryssa Hart, I'm not taking your enticing money, and fuck me because I'm going to sit in that rathole and stay proud but poor. Purity. There has to be some way out of this. Maybe I am hung up on false pride. Carrie don't even make $1,500 a year, and she won't take welfare or anything, not even from the church. Maybe it runs in the family. Family, now that's a fat laugh. What family? All I had was room and board. Well, some of it rubbed off, I guess. But it's more than poor pride. If that woman loved me it'd be different or if I loved her. I'd take anything she gave me then, but she don't give a flying fuck about me. She buys me the way she goes and buys a winter coat or a Gucci handbag. I'm a piece of meat. Damn, I go walking down the street and the men look at me like a walking sperm receptacle. I walk into a party and this buzzard sees flesh. She's no different from a construction worker, she's just got class and bread, that's all.

Well, piss, I'm not sittin' here on this Goddamn subway train feeling sorry for myself. Fuck that shit. So an old dyke tries to buy my ass. Big deal. So I'm eating the wallpaper off the walls and ripping off day-old bread. Tough shit. I am getting my ass over to N.Y.U. tomorrow and telling those academic robots that they're giving me a scholarship. I'm the hottest thing since Eisenstein; they're lucky to be able to help me in my formative stage. Hell, there's more than one way to skin a cat. Carrie all the time said that. Shit, I wish I'd stop thinking about Carrie.

After months of bureaucratic shuffle and a battery
of entrance exams I won a tuition scholarship.
I took classes during the day and worked at The
Flick at night. Holly only saw me on weekends
and didn't take to my schedule kindly nor did she
take film school seriously.

One weekend night we were mobbed at work.
The place was jammed with middle-aged, white,
suburban theater goers and preppies who couldn't
get into the Playboy Club and had to settle for
imitation bunnies. We worked four tables each.
It was near the end of our shift and we were all
tired.

One of Holly's tables emptied and a sallow
man, maybe forty-five sat down with a plump
wife in her green satin dress that was near to
busting at her hips. My tables were eating and
contented, so I had a little breathing space. Holly

whizzed by, tray in the air, running down to the kitchen to get the couple's order. She returned with one orange freeze and an enormous banana split—six scoops of ice cream, mountains of whipped cream, three different syrups, and an obese cherry that bordered on the obscene.

The little man watched Holly, actually he never took his eyes off her perfect breasts. She served the wife first and as the lady imprisoned in green satin with her metallic hair peered at her sweetheart straw wrapper, the husband reached right up and fondled Holly's left breast. He's loaded I thought, this guy has got to be loaded. Holly took a step back to view him more clearly, then she carefully put the banana split in her right hand and smashed it on his head. The entire top floor of The Flick broke out in a chorus of laughter and noise. He bellowed and jumped out of his metal chair, knocked it over and fell on his ass. His wife, seeing him on the floor with an enormous cherry oozing down his hairy ear, released a splitting wail, "Harold, there's a cherry on your ear!"

Harold would have had a banana in his ear if Holly could have gotten a good hold on him. She kicked him in the balls, grabbed him by the scruff of the neck and, dragged him to the top of the stairway. There she put her foot firmly on his rear and launched him without countdown. He collided into the manager, who was huffing his two hundred and fifty pounds up the stairs looking like an ad for the heart association fund.

"What's the meaning of this?" Larry the Leech squawked, his affected masculine voice lost in the hysteria of the moment.

"That putrid prick laid his hand on my breast, that's what's the meaning of this."

By now people were out of their seats crowding around the stairway for a better view. I was standing directly behind Holly. Larry's face was mottled red and he reached down to help the tit tweaker to his feet. Whipped cream and remnants of syrupy banana covered the carpet.

"You're fired, now get outa here. I'm sorry, Sir, this is most unfortunate." Larry then looked at me and, remembering that Holly and I were friends, added as a postscript, "You can stay, I'm not mad at you."

Holly whirled around and jacked her foot squarely in Larry's huge gut. He sailed down the stairs, airborne without a sound until he bombed on the bottom step. She locked my wrist in an iron clasp and announced at the top of her lungs, "If I'm fired, I'm taking my wife with me!"

The uproar was louder than a home run at the World Series. Holly yanked me down the steps and out into the street. She didn't let go until we had walked to the Lexington Avenue subway. I was a mixture of amazement and laughter.

"You shook the shit out of all of them, but Holly, you told a lie, we're not married. Now all those nice people will think I'm taken. This is the ruin of my single life."

She was still too wrought up to be amused. "Shut up and come home with me."

"I can't. I have to get up early tomorrow and go to the library to do some research on D. W. Griffith. Come down to my place."

"Go to that dump?"

"Well, I'm in it so close your eyes to the rest."

"All right, but don't wake me up when you go to the library."

We rode down to the apartment in silence. The crosstown at Union Square took forever so we walked down Fourteenth Street all the way to the river and up to the apartment. Holly wasn't cooled by the walk, it only irritated her more. As I opened the door and heard the police lock click into place, I turned on the light accompanied by Holly's "How can you live in this rathole? You're a fool not to let Chryssa keep you."

"Let's not get into that. I've got enough on my mind. Glad as I was to see both that little shriveled-up turd get it and Larry too, now I've got to look for another job."

"Look, you stubborn shit, if you'd just bend a little you wouldn't have to kill yourself like this— and you'd have some clothes, a decent apartment, a few little lovelies that make life easier."

"Holly, lay off."

"Lay off what? You think you're too good to be kept? I'm kept, so what am I, a whore or something? Or maybe it's symptomatic of my race's refusal to be responsible. That what you think?"

"No. We're different people and it has nothing to do with whoring or color or any of that shit. I can't do it, that's that."

"Don't hand me that shit. You can't do it because you're a fucking prude and you think it's immoral. Well, I think you're a goddamn ass, that's what I think. You spent your whole life in poverty and now you have a chance to have something. Take it."

"You don't understand, Holly, I don't want to live here. I don't want raggedy clothes. I don't want to be running on nerves for the next ten years, but I have to do it my way. My way, understand. It has nothing to do with morality, it has to do with me."

"Oh, come off it, Horatio Alger."

"I don't want a fight. Can't we forget it for tonight?"

"No, I'm not going to forget it because I know you're making a value judgment on me."

"I am *not*. Now stop trying to guilt trip me."

"You think I'm weak and lazy, don't you? You think I'm a soft rich kid who's taking money from her lover instead of from doctor daddy. Why don't you say it? You don't love me."

"I never said I did."

Holly blinked and then her eyes narrowed. "Why, you can't fall in love with a decadent, middle-class, black brat?"

"Just stop, will you? This is ridiculous."

"Ridiculous, I'll tell you what's ridiculous. You sitting here in this, working yourself to the bone and for what—to be a film director. Listen to me, baby: big dreams, big dreams. You can graduate at the top of your class. You probably will, but you're not going to get any work. You're another piece of ass who can sit in a secretary's chair with your Phi Beta Kappa key wrapped around your neck. You're doing all this for nothing. You know what, you're a lot like my father. I never realized that until now. He worked his ass off too and he got rich but he wanted to go all the way to the top and he's not getting there for the obvious reason. You two would make a fine pair, bullheaded, can't see what's coming down in front of you. Gonna fight the whole world and get nothing but kicked in the ass. At least, my old man got money out of the deal. You aren't even going to get that. You'd better grab on to Chryssa Hart because she's the best you'll get, honey."

"Goddammit! No matter what happens to me I'll still have the knowledge inside my head and nobody can take that away from me. And someday, even if you can't see it coming, I'm going to make use of that knowledge and make my movies. My movies, you hear me, Holly—not soppy romances about hapless heterosexuals, not family dramas about sparkling white America, not Westerns that run red from first reel to last or science fiction thrillers where renegade white corpuscles fill the screen—my movies, real movies about real people and about the way the shit comes down. Now if I don't get the money to do that until I'm fifty, then that's the way it is. I'm doing this so help me God and it's not for nothing."

"You know, you're incredible. I don't know if you're crazy or if you're the stuff that towers over the masses of the mediocre, but I'm not going to stick around to find out. I'm not willing to have to watch you go through the ugliness you're going through now and I don't think I could face what's going to happen after this—when all those doors shut in your face and they tell you whatever lie it is they're telling to Blacks and Puerto Ricans and women that day. You're strong enough to take it, but I'm not strong enough to watch it. After watching Daddy, I haven't got the heart to see it all over again." She stopped, took a breath and lowered her eyes to the linoleum floor, "I feel shitty. I just feel shitty. Maybe some of it is that

I don't have real work of my own. I go around being beautiful and having fun, yeah, but I don't have anything for me, really mine, and you do, and it fucking kills me."

"So what the hell am I supposed to do? Give it up to make you happy? Be a failure, so you can feel good about yourself?"

"No, no. Oh, Molly, deep inside I do want you to bust right out of here, to break the whole scene wide open. I know what it means to you, and maybe I'm even perceptive enough to know what it will mean to a lot of other people if you do. It's the everyday wear and tear that brings out the green in me. I begin to hate you, hate you and I love you, that's a fucked mess—but I start to resent you for all the things that make you strong, that enable you to stand up under that daily erosion. I begin to hate myself because I'm not like you. I don't know, maybe it was because my parents gave me everything, spoiled me, maybe that's why I've got no drive."

"There were plenty of people who had things given to them, who were middle-class, who had drive."

"So what. I don't care what they did. I care about what I'm going to do. What the hell am I going to do with my life? Tell me what to do?"

"I can't. It wouldn't mean anything if I told you. You got to tell you."

"It's so hard."

"For Christ's sake, it's always hard no matter who you are, where you came from, what color your skin happens to be or what sex you got stuck with. It's the hardest decision every individual has to make in their life, probably."

"Yeah, I know. I know it's hard where you're at right now and I'm not doing you any good with my emphasis on the pleasure principle."

"And I know it's hard where you're at, too. I'm sorry."

"Me too, I'm sorry I yelled at you and I'm sorry I lost you the job. I'm such a dumb shit. I have to go off and get my head together. Maybe I'll ask Kim for the money to go to Paris for a couple of months or maybe I'll go to Ethiopia—I have a friend there from college. It might be easier to make up my mind if I'm out of this insane city."

"You can make up your mind anywhere, even in jail. Going to Paris sounds like a ritzy cop-out."

"Fuck you. You have to throw in my face that you don't have that option, don't you. People like you make me sick, wearing your poverty like a badge of purity."

"I didn't mean it to sound that way. Maybe I did sound self-righteous. Well, hell, I'd like to go to Paris myself or wherever. But all I'm trying to say is, don't make a ritual out of getting your head together, that's all."

"Yeah, okay. I can't tell anymore if you're putting me down or being level. I get pissed off at you a lot these days. I guess we're out of phase, you know. Maybe one of the ways I'll get myself together is not to see you for awhile."

"If that's the way you feel about it, then that's the way it has to be."

"You don't seem very upset."

"Goddammit, woman, I'm doing the best I can to help you do whatever it is you have to do. No, I'm not crushed. Do you want me to be crushed and fizzle in a puddle at your feet like the Witch of the West? And yes, I will miss you. I'll miss making love with you and going to the Thalia and you're probably the only woman I'll ever know who kicked a fat pig down the stairs when she's in total drag. Okay?"

"Oh shit, I do love you. I do." She picked up her cape, slid open the police lock, and closed the door behind her. I listened to her footsteps until she opened and closed the front door. She strode to the corner and hailed a cab. I watched until she tucked her feet in and closed the door.

I set out among the subways, the red-and-white
Coke machines and ads for Dr. Scholl's foot
powder to find another job. Night work ran in two
categories: telephone operating or various forms
of entertainment. Since Hal Prince did not rush
out on the street to sign me up I found myself
dancing nightly in a bar in the West Fifties. That
lasted two weeks—until I provided a dentist with
a patient needing a new set of uppers. There was
nothing to do but change my schedule, cut down
on classes, and work during the day.

I got a job as a secretary at Silver Publishing
Company. Every morning at nine a.m. I roared
into the office in complete female rig—skirt,
stockings, slip. I couldn't cross my legs because
some of the more obvious sperm producers would
try to look up my leg, couldn't put my feet on the
desk because that wasn't ladylike, and if I didn't

wear make-up everyone, including the boss, would ask me if I was "under the weather" that day.

My immediate superior was Stella by Starlight. Stella had married the president of the company, David Cohen, so she worked "just for fun." Stella looked exactly like Ruby Keeler and someone must have told her this back in 1933 because she had been trying ever since to be a carbon copy of the original. At the merest suggestion of Ruby she'd go into the routine from *Footlight Parade*. Then, her husband, aroused by the sound of tapping feet, would have to come out of his office to remind her there were galleys to be read and would she save the dance until after five.

We lowlies were herded into the bullpen where we cheerlessly typed up anything from a bill to the latest manuscript as well as churning out back-copy, front-copy, and captions for bent photo-graphs. In a short time Stella managed to notice that I could both read and spell, two points in my favor, joined by a remarkable third: I could dash off copy on command. Stella rescued me from the bullpen and threw me in with one of the prized editors, James Adler.

Rhea Rhadin, another groundling who had fought her way up to being head receptionist, un-fortunately had a full blown heterosexual crush on James. She'd practically slide into the office on her own lubrication and croon at him, "James, may I fetch you some coffee—anything at all this morning?" James abhored her and gave her a curt "no" on these persistent occasions. Rhea exhibited the peculiar twists so often found in the brains of straight women: she became convinced that James treated her brusquely because he and I were having a hot fling. She decided to make life miserable for me. Any work she got from my hands she deliberately botched and then blamed it on me. Once a week she would slip into Mr. Cohen's office with another horrendous mistake she had saved the printer from committing because of my laxity and poor work habits. James in an heroic effort to save me reported his perceptions of the situation to Mr. Cohen, who couldn't believe anyone, even Rhea, could be such an ass.

A bad case of the hots was only one of Rhea's faults. She was notoriously lazy and connived to get other luckless lowlies to do her job for her, thereby giving her time to file her fingernails and change the color of the polish daily. Mr. Cohen turned a blind eye to her eternal manicure by saying we should be kind to her, after all her mother did kill herself when Rhea was eleven. The situation grew daily more intolerable, and so the mixture of loneliness since Holly left and the irritation at work gave birth to a scheme I was sure would do old Rhea Ratface in. Sunday night I went out with a plastic garbage bag and collected every agreeable specimen of dogshit I could find. I got half a bagful and I carefully twisted the candy-striped red wire and put it next to my briefcase for tomorrow's labor.

Seven in the morning I was dragging that damn bag through the subway station, up the stairs, and into the square office building streaked with grime, pigeon patties, and car exhaust. By eight I had feverishly crammed the presents into Rhea's desk drawers. Then I evacuated by the back stairway and didn't come back until 9:10.

Rhea was at her desk, Revlon's Mocha Mist by her right hand, the telephone in her left, chattering away as usual. Mr. Cohen came in with Stella trailing after him at 9:20. Rhea was still on the phone. James and I were working on a book about medieval art when Rhea paraded through the open door, "Really, James, I don't see why you and Miss Bolt have to sit so close together when you work. Photographs of Flemish churches can't be that interesting."

"Rhea, don't you have some work to do?" James muttered.

"Yes, I was taking a little break. Would you like some coffee?"

"No, thank you."

She oozed away, thoroughly happy that she had needled her love. Through the open door I could see her plopped at her desk behind the glass partition on the phone again. She hadn't cracked a desk drawer. The entire morning crept along and she never opened even one drawer.

James and I were having lunch in the office, because we had an enormous amount of copy to cover before the author came in at 3:00. As if sensing we were in a hurry, Stella sashayed into the office and noticed James eating a Hershey almond bar.

"I thought you were on a diet. What's the matter, are you tired of eggs and tuna fish? You know eggs cause special acids and mucus in your system."

"No, I didn't know that but—"

Stella cut him off, "Dave has a little yellow pill that clears it right up. No mucus problems for him. I made him go to the doctor, Dr. Bronstein, the one who says I'm the spitting image of Ruby Keeler. Bronstein says there's not a thing wrong with Dave but he should take the pill for his drip. You should see the doctor about a diet. I had a friend who went to a special clinic for her weight. All she ate was grapes and watermelon. After three days she felt much lighter. Grapes and watermelon."

James rallied a smile, after all you can't tell the boss's wife to fuck off. "I loathe watermelon, although I like them pickled."

"Yes, I like pickled watermelons, too, Did you ever have mushmelons? I like those a lot. I bought a mushmelon before Dave left for Chicago. When did he go there? September? Well, I bought a mushmelon in September, but it wasn't ripe so I put it in my refrigerator and as soon as it got ripe I ate it. I ate a little bit of it each day. It was wonderful not to have to cook for Dave and just pick at mushmelon. He's so fussy that it's a relief when he goes on these little trips. Our refrigerator is full of oranges. He won't drink anything but freshly-squeezed orange juice. Today I was naughty and reveled in not washing out the squeezer." James looked up wearily from a colored photograph of Henry the II's heaven cloak and started again to try to indicate she should leave but Stella shifted into second gear and ran him down: "Mr. Cohen has to have his orange juice fresh and everything just so. He won't sit down to the table if I put luncheon napkins next to his plate when he has breakfast. I have to keep three sizes of napkins around the house to please him. We bought new cereal bowls and he complained that I gave him too much cereal, so I had to pour the cereal in the old bowl then pour it in the new bowl in front of him before he was satisfied. But coffee brings out the worst in him. He is pickier about his coffee than he is about these manuscripts."

"That's impossible," James asserted.

"Ha. If you think he's hard as a boss, you should live with him." Stella, realizing what she had said, took a step back and peeped around the door to make certain no one had heard such blasphemy. "James, I have to grind the beans myself for him. First, I have to run after him with orange juice. Then he sits at the table and inspects the napkins and demands to see the cereal measured. Then he demands his coffee and each morning there's something wrong with it. After all this activity it's 9:10 and he says to me, 'Hurry up, we'll be late,' and I haven't even had a cup of coffee or orange juice myself." As she inhaled for a refueling we were saved by an ear-splitting shriek from behind the glass partition.

"Shit! Shit! My desk is full of shit. Every drawer has turds and crap and yuk in it."

From down at the end of the longest corridor in the office's dull grid structure you could hear running feet. People swarmed out of their cubicles which had pictures of Chiquita banana on the wall. In the press by Rhea's desk, her photograph of Rhett Butler was rubbed off the wall.

Stella blustered to the front of the mob. "Rhea, what terrible language, what's the . . ." Before

she could finish she was rendered speechless for
the first time in her long life by the sight of all
that carefully arranged dogshit. The ruckus drew
Mr. Cohen out of a conference and he slammed
the door behind him for full effect. The crowd
parted for their patriarch like the Red Sea.

"What the hell is going on out here? Rhea,
what's the matter with you?"

Rhea, her face bloated with rage, spat out,
"My desk is full of dogshit."

David Cohen with impeccable logic answered
in a calm, fatherly voice, "But that's impossible.
There are no dogs in this office."

Stella nudged her husband's shoulder. "Look
in her desk, Dave."

He briefly glanced toward the drawers, turned
his head and bent over for a second look then he
said to his wife in a little voice, "But that's impossible."

Stella held her ground, "Impossible or not, her
desk is filled with dog . . . uh, droppings."

"This must be someone's idea of a joke," Dave
concluded. "Whoever did this should apologize
to Rhea immediately and clean up this mess."
Silence. Utter silence. "Maybe it's one of the
Puerto Ricans in the shipping room. It's absurd
to think anyone in the front office would do such
a thing." Armed with his new conclusion, forti-
fied with the knowledge that men who don't wear
coats and ties are capable of any crime, he turned
on his heel and started for shipping. From the
shipping room we could hear excited voices in
Spanish. David Cohen came back looking confused and angry.

"All right. Back to work, people. This is a publishing house not a circus. The janitor will clean up this mess."

Rhea by the time of the boss's return had worked up a good cry. Melted by the sight of this unfortunate in tears, Mr. Cohen gave her the rest of the day off. James and I had settled back over the manuscript when Rhea came in.

"It was you, Molly. I know it was you. Only a lesbian would stoop to such a thing. Did you know that, James? Your girlfriend is a dyke. She told me so herself. But you're even lower than a lesbian, Molly Bolt. You're a lesbian who steals men!" As she was ranting and waving her arms her pocketbook, which was half open, opened all the way when she had it on the upswing and her bag of wares rained on the floor. For a lazy girl she moved fast but not fast enough. James had picked up her birth control pills.

"Give me those."

"Delighted to, dear Rhea, but don't take them on my account."

Hell hath no fury like a woman who has been told she doesn't need her daily dosage of uterine cancer by the man she loves. Rhea took a swing at James with her full-loaded and prudently-closed purse. He ducked and she gave up with another earsplitting shriek and ran out the door directly into Polina Bellantoni, author of *The Creative Spirit of the Middle Ages*, who was right on time for her afternoon appointment. James and I broke for the door where we each took an arm and raised the woman to her feet.

Polina Bellantoni was firm of flesh, at least her arm was in good shape. She was forty-one years old, had been married twenty years, had mothered a child who was sixteen and had managed to raise the daughter while completing her Ph.D. in Babylonian underpants for Columbia University. Currently, she was teaching at Columbia having left ancient fashions for medieval studies. Polina's hair was blue-black with strands of perfect, electric gray and her eyes were a soft brown. Wrinkles played around those eyes and made her look both knowing and beautiful. I realized in a flash that men were total fools to put middle-aged women out to pasture for a smooth and boring strawberry face. I don't know about love at first sight, but I decided right then and there to bridge the generation gap. Somehow, someway, someday I was going to love this married lady with the sixteen-year-old daughter and camelback trucks filled with remnants of archaic undies.

Every two weeks Polina showed up at the office. She was the nervous type and double-checked everything that James and I did. This drove James right up the wall, so I volunteered to take care of matters. Every other Thursday Polina and I went over manuscript changes, photographs and captions. She was impressed that I was so careful with her work and amazed that I was going to school while working full-time. On her fourth visit she asked me if I'd like to have dinner with her family.

On the night of the dinner I showed up in the best clothes I could piece together. She lived in a spacious apartment overlooking Morningside Heights. After meeting me at the door she deposited me in the living room with her husband, while she went back to the kitchen. Mr. Bellantoni treated me like a student, giving me those fatherly smiles and calculated pauses in his delivery. You're supposed to smile during those pauses. He had earned his Ph.D. in art history. His original thesis was cataloging cows in nineteenth century French paintings and he had expanded this original interest to a thorough knowledge of cows in Western art. This very summer he had been invited to deliver the definitive paper on this subject to a group of his esteemed colleagues at Cambridge, England. Soon, he confided, leaning over to draw me into his words, he would begin his greatest project: cows in Indian art—a long smoldering passion.

He was forty-nine, paunchy, with sagging red cheeks already betraying age spots. I forgot his name. But Alice, the daughter of the cow man and the underpants woman was unforgettable. Her complexion radiated sweetness and her almond eyes were a pure, piercing green. Alice's hair hung down to her ass and changed from brown to honey to ash at the tips. Her large breasts stood straight out without benefit of a bra. Alice was a Renaissance princess come back to life.

Polina was delighted that her daughter and I could talk. Mostly we talked about Janis Joplin, the Moody Blues and Aretha Franklin—things Polina never heard about other than to yell at Alice to turn her stereo down. Polina rarely left Babylon except to vacation in the tenth century. But on those sparse moments when she peeked into the present, she seemed to enjoy me.

Polina asked her husband questions throughout our meal to try to get him to act alive but mouth to mouth couldn't have revived him. After dinner he wandered back into his den, the obligatory pipe dangling out of his mouth.

The three of us sat around a brass coffee table. Polina told me about Hrosvitha, a tenth-century German nun who wrote plays in crystal clear Latin. She played with Alice's hair and continued her tale of the nun. Her Latin was as good as Terence's, the Roman playwright. And that was so pure that no one would believe a woman could write such perfect verse. It was a raging controversy in the medieval scholars' world, equal to the controversy over black intelligence in the psychology world. There was something pathetic about all that intelligence of hers squandered in the murky past and defined by the dusty priorities of academic life. But she was intelligent, and I had lived long enough to know that's cause for celebration.

My triumph of the evening was in picking up a copy of Hrosvitha's "Dulcitius" and reading it right off the page, in cadence.

"That's lovely. Your Latin is lovely."

"Thank you. I studied it all through high school and I'm still at it in college. I'm reading Livy and Tacitus these days with a little Attic Greek thrown in for good measure."

Polina clapped her hands and gave me a bear hug. "No wonder you've been so helpful to me! You're a classics scholar. We're a rare breed these days, you know. Ever since they took Latin off the compulsory study list in high schools, we've been slipping. But I find that only the brightest kids keep on with Latin. That's good, I guess."

"Well, I'm not really a classics scholar. I'm

in film studies. I take Latin and Greek for the language credit, but I love them."

"I hope so. Greek is too difficult to take for laughs. If you're in film studies, why Latin and Greek?"

"Uh—this may sound funny to you, but Latin especially has helped my ability to discipline myself more than anything I've ever studied. It wouldn't matter what I would do, Latin would help me because it taught me how to think. And Greek, that adds a soaring quality, something that pushed my mind fast. I—well, this must sound stupid to you."

"No, no, not at all. I think that's exactly right about Latin teaching you the process of logic, to think, I mean. Too bad a few more of our politicians haven't studied it."

Alice was sitting wide-eyed through all this. "Molly, is that true about the Latin or are you buttering the old lady up?" She ribbed her mother and Polina grabbed her hand and held it.

"No. I know it sounds weird but it was the best thing I ever studied. I take that back. Not the best thing, but the most useful."

Alice moved forward on her seat, "Mom has been at me to take Latin so I did this year. I hate it. But maybe that's because my teacher is a fossil."

"Latin teachers have a way of getting ossified."

"Mine is pickled! Have you made any movies yet?"

"A two-minute flick last semester. I have a hard time getting to the equipment, because I'm the only woman in the class and well, the men don't like that much. Since other men control the equipment sign-out, I always get screwed."

Polina's eyebrows went together. Wrong word, I guess. "That's disgraceful. Isn't there anything you can do about it?"

"I file complaints with the head of the department with clockwork punctuality. But he hates women. He brings me into his office, reads over the complaint. Then he says he'll check into it and nothing happens. Naturally this doesn't make me feel great, but worse. All through his lectures he makes rotten cracks about women. You know, the stud routine about the reason there haven't been any great women directors is because we have brains the size of peas—and he looks right at me when he says that. Makes me want to cram a can of *Triumph of the Will* right down his throat."

Polina sighed and traced a circle on the edge of her coffee cup. "It doesn't get much easier when you're out. This year I should have been made an associate professor, but they're still keeping me at assistant."

"Oh Mom, you'll get it. You're the best there is. These twentieth-century Victorians have to give in sometime."

Polina stroked her hair and smiled at her. "We'll see."

After that dinner, Polina and I began to see each other once a week. We'd go to galleries, museums, lectures, and every now and then she'd take me to a play. Polina detested musicals so she'd only take me to see straight drama. Mostly it was awful except for the APA Repertory.

Polina took me to *School for Scandal*. It was so quick, light, and well acted that we left the theater stoned on the joy of it.

"That was wonderful, simply wonderful. Makes me want to dance," Polina giggled.

"I know a place where we can dance if you want to?"

"And stand around waiting for some buffoon to ask us to dance? Never."

"You can dance with me unless, of course, I fit the buffoon slot."

"What?" Her hair flew around her head as she turned to eye me.

"Oh, you really think I'm a dolt. Aha, the truth comes out."

"Not at all. Where can we dance together?"

"In a lesbian bar, where else?"

"How do you know about a lesbian bar?"

"I'm a lesbian."

"You—but you look like anyone else. Molly, don't be silly; you can't be a lesbian. You're joking. I'd know if you were such a thing."

"Madam, I am a full-blooded, bona fide lesbian. As for the way I look, most lesbians I know look like any other woman. However, if you're hot for a truck driver I know just the place." I couldn't resist giving her that little dig.

For two entire blocks we walked in silence. Polina's bouyancy had evaporated. "If you don't mind, Molly, I think I'll go home. I'm more worn out than I suspected."

"Of course I mind. Why don't you tell the truth? You're upset because I told you I'm gay."

She avoided my eyes. "Yes."

"What difference does it make? Tell me. I'm

the exact, same person you knew before. Jesus Christ, I'll never understand straight people!"

"Please, let me go home and think this through." She darted into the subway station at 42nd Street and I walked the whole way home. Walking helps me calm down, but when I put the key in my lock I was as upset as when I started. Why does it get to me? Why can't I just write off those people the way they write me off? Why does it always get through and hurt?

15

For three solid weeks Polina kept her distance. No Thursday visits to the office, no phone calls, no anything. Just blanket silence. I was determined not to call her. She told me that she had a male lover. Paul Digita, who taught English at New York University. Out of curiosity I decided to see what he looked like. I knew beforehand that he was crippled. His left leg dragged after him and he had to use a cane. He had balked on the pole vault at Exeter in 1949 and bent his leg permanently out of shape. Even so, I wasn't ready for him when I laid eyes on him. The leg was the least of his problems. He was myopic, had a wicked case of dandruff, and it looked as though he was hosting an algae colony on his teeth. Paul was a living study in human debris. How could she be turned on to this? What could they possibly have in common? After his lecture on

Yeats' use of the semicolon, I forced myself to go up to him and tell him how much I enjoyed it. The flattery nearly knocked him over; he held on to the side of the podium or maybe his leg was giving out. Anyway, he offered to take me to tea and I accepted although it took nerves of steel to look him right in the face, algae and all.

Over a cup of overpriced tea, Paul told me he was a misunderstood genius. In fact, Paul spared me no detail of his life. He didn't ask me anything about myself. Two hours later exhausted from his endless personal narrative, he asked if he might see me again.

I actually told this ugly blob of protoplasm, yes. God. So we set a date for next week. Polina had no idea to what lengths I was willing to go and neither did I.

Before my date with Paul, Polina called. She was sorry. Naturally, my lesbianism shouldn't make any difference and after many visits to her psychiatrist, who after all saved her emotional life back in 1963, she came to the earth-shattering conclusion that it was okay for me to be whatever I wanted to be as long as I had adjusted as a mature, healthy human being. She complimented me on being a mature and healthy human being and would I like to see a movie with her this Friday?

We saw *Wait Until Dark* and it scared the bejesus out of both of us. My apartment was right by the Elgin Theater so I asked her if she wanted a drink before going home. Polina hesitated for a moment then her courage got the better of her and she said that would be lovely. She was appalled but too polite to say it as she huffed her way up my rickety, unlit, tenement steps. And when she saw my apartment with only a mattress on raised milk cartons and more brightly painted milk cartons all over the place, she was astounded.

"You're so imaginative. You've made charming little bookcases and chairs out of milk cartons."

"Thank you. I have an unopened bottle of Lancer's wine that I've been saving for a special occasion—why don't we open that?"

"That would be fine."

The wine went directly to Polina's tongue and she told me how freaked out she was and how secretly she thought lesbianism attracted and frightened every woman, because every woman could be a lesbian, but it was all hidden and unknown. Did I get into it because of the allure of the forbidden? She then went on to say what a wonderful relationship she had with her husband. They had an understanding about Paul, and wasn't heterosexuality just grand?

"It bores me, Polina."

"Bores you—what do you mean?"

"I mean men bore me. If one of them behaves like an adult it's cause for celebration, and even when they do act human, they still aren't as good in bed as women."

"Maybe you haven't met the right man?"

"Maybe you haven't met the right woman. And I bet I've slept with more men than you have, and they all work the same show. Some are better at it than others but it's boring once you know what women are like."

"You can't sit there and say a thing like that about men."

"Okay, then I won't say anything. Better to shut my mouth than lie about it."

A disturbed pause. "What's so different about sleeping with women? I mean, exactly what is the difference?"

"For one thing, it's more intense."

"You don't think things between men and women get intense?"

"Of course they do but it's not the same, that's all!"

"How?"

"Oh, lady, there aren't words for it. I don't know—it's the difference between a pair of roller skates and a Ferrari—ah, there aren't words."

"I think the lady doth protest too much. You wouldn't promote such blatant lesbian propaganda if you were sure of yourself and your sexual identity."

"Propaganda? I took a few minutes to try to answer a question you asked me. If you want to see blatant propaganda then look at the ads in the subways, magazines, t.v., everywhere. The big pigs use heterosexuality and women's bodies to sell everything in this country—even violence. Damn, you people are so bad off you got to have computers to match you up these days."

Polina began to get angry, but then she took some time to think about what I had laid on her. "I never thought of it that way, I mean about advertising and all."

"Well, I sure have. You don't see ads of women kissing to get you to buy Salem cigarettes, do you?"

She laughed. "That's funny, that's truly funny. Why the entire world must look different to you."

"It does. It looks destructive, diseased, and corroded. People have no selves anymore (maybe they never had them in the first place) so their home base is their sex—their genitals, who they fuck. It's enough to make a chicken laugh."

"I—are all homosexuals as perceptive as you?"

"I don't know. I haven't talked to all homosexuals." Polina had sense enough to be embarrassed about that last question. She paused long enough to finish her glass, then reload. She was getting stewed. "Maybe you should switch to soda. I don't want you to get tanked."

"Me, no, I'm fine. I'll sip this"—and she gulped down half of it. She began to frankly stare at me. I liked Polina, maybe I even loved her a little, but this was hard to take. I didn't expect such an intelligent woman to be so classic a heterosexual bigot. I felt like a bug under a magnifying glass. Oh well, maybe the only beauty left in cities is in the oil slicks on the road and maybe there isn't any beauty left in the people who live in these places.

Polina interrupted this grim line of thought. "Molly, have you slept with many women?"

"Hundreds. I'm irresistible."

"Be serious."

"I am serious—I'm irresistible." I reached over, putting my hands on her shoulders and gave her a kiss that startled both of us. She began to pull away but then decided to stick it out. Noble and daring of her. Predictably, she had to protest after the kiss.

"You shouldn't have done that. I don't see that you're any different from a man, coming over here and kissing me like that without asking."

"If I had asked you, you wouldn't have kissed me. Here, let me give you another one, so you can be sure to know the difference. I'd hate to have you confuse me with the opposite gender."

Her eyes widened and she started to balk, but I wasn't in a sympathetic mood. I held her tight and delivered a long French kiss. She loved it. She loved it and hated me for making her love it. She broke away in a full fury. "How dare you! How dare you—why I'm old enough to be your mother."

"I'm old enough to know that doesn't make any difference. Why don't you climb off your sanctified prick. You dig it. Anyone with half a vagina left would dig it. Women kissing women is beautiful. And women making love together is dynamite. So why don't you just let yourself go and get into it."

"This is outrageous. You're a lunatic."

"That's a distinct possibility but at least I know what I'm talking about from practical experience. You only know one side of the story—"

That one hurt her. It was too close to home. I was a good five inches shorter than Polina, but that didn't stop me from going over and bodily putting her on my mattress. Before she could double up her soft hands to belt me, I gave her another kiss. And I touched her breast, pressed her thighs, and Polina decided that she didn't know the other side of the story and forty-one years is a long time in the dark. So here she was and how convenient it was too because I had half forced her into it. This way she could avoid responsibility for making love with another woman; the wine helped a lot on that account, too. But she kissed me back for whatever reasons. She stretched out on the mattress and pushed right into my body. There wasn't much to say. As soon as we both had our clothes off and were under the covers she looked at me with clever eyes and said, "Where are we?"

"What?"

"Where are we?"

"We're in bed, in my apartment. Where else could we be?"

"No, no, we're in a men's john."

"We are?"

"Yes, we're both at the urinal in the Times Square subway station."

"Polina, they wouldn't let us use the men's john."

"You have to tell this story with me. You have to play out this fantasy or I can't come. So please, now we're at the urinal and you look over and notice my cock and you say, 'That's a nice cock, big and juicy.—well, say it!"

"That's a—nice cock"—cough—"big and juicy."

She started to get excited and wiggle on the bed. "Go on, go on."

"What do I say next?"

"Tell me anything. You make it up."

"Uh—that's the juiciest cock I've ever seen. It's a real biggie."

Harshly, "Ask me if you can touch it."

"May I touch your cock, please?"

Polina gave a low moan. "Oh yes, touch it and kiss it and suck on it." And she came right then and there as I told her I wanted to hold it, kiss it, and suck on it.

After a ten-minute reflection period, she rolled over and said, "Do you want me to make love to you? I've never done it before but I'm sure I can."

"Yes, I'd like it if you'd make love to me."

"What fantasy do you have?"

"I don't think I have any."

"But how can you make love without a fantasy? Everyone has sexual fantasies. I bet it's something you think is too awful to tell. You can tell me. It'll make me all excited again."

"I'm sorry but I just like to make love. It's the touching and the kissing and all that gets me turned on. You wouldn't have to say a word."

"I don't believe anyone in this day and age can live without a fantasy."

"Well, I do have one thing but I'm not sure it's a fantasy."

"Tell, tell." She put her arm around my waist.

"When I make love to women I think of their genitals as a, as a ruby fruit jungle."

"Ruby fruit jungle?"

"Yeah, women are thick and rich and full of hidden treasures and besides that, they taste good."

"That's hardly a fantasy. You have an extremely immature sex life, Molly. No wonder you're a lesbian."

"If it's all the same with you I think I could do without being made love to."

"Oh, you're embarrassed because you don't have a fantasy. Don't be. I'll make one up for you. I do want to make love to you. You have a very sexy body—it's light and smooth and tight. You're Plato's perfect androgen. No, that's not right—

203

you're a woman without fail. But you're so strong. You haven't got flab anywhere. I—I want to go inside of you. It must be exciting to go inside another woman where she's wet and open."

"Okay, okay, you make up the story and I'll listen while you make love to me."

Polina made up a story about being students at a boys' boarding school. In this one we did it in the locker room. It turned her on so much that she made love to me with absolute frenzy. But I could sense Polina and I weren't going to have much of a relationship. I couldn't survive the stories, and I couldn't understand why they were about men.

She didn't spend the night although I wanted her to. It's nice to curl up next to a warm body, then wake up in the morning for a hello hug. But she said she had to sleep with her old blue sweater on and a big pillow under her knees. She couldn't possibly sleep in the same bed with another human being. So she went home and I couldn't sleep the whole night trying to figure out if I dreamed it or if it was true. It was true. The next morning when a little bit of sunlight fought its way through the pollution to my mattress I found some long strands of black hair and a few gray ones.

My date with Paul turned up and I went, out of a sense of blazing curiosity. What could these two do? Did he tell her these absurd stories? There was only one way to find out.

Paul took me to an Italian restaurant and then fumbled for the next move. He obviously wasn't used to female attention and was at loose ends.

I suggested we walk in Riverside Park for awhile. I told him I'd walk him home since he lived right on the Park. It took us one half hour to go four blocks. We arrived at his door and he started to hobble in, then turned as if struck by a blinding thought. "Would you like to come upstairs and look at my thesis? It was highly regarded at Harvard."

"I'd love to see your thesis."

Paul spent the next hour and one half explaining to me the supreme importance of punctuation in early twentieth-century poetry. He worked himself into a lather over the horrible idea that poetry was ditching punctuation. After this diatribe he took a swig of Squirt and vodka and started a tirade against Edmund Wilson. Without warning he stopped talking, lurched off his side of the sofa and kissed me—with those teeth. Jesus. Before I had time to get myself geared he dove into my crotch like he was right out of *Dawn Patrol* and he slobbered all over me. Paul didn't believe in warming up.

"Paul, why don't we go into your bedroom?"

"Oh, right."

Once in his bedroom I was greeted with fresh horrors. Every inch of him was covered in hair. Right out of the trees he dropped and into my crotch. I must be in love with Polina to endure this orangutan. God. Paul was jabbering and rolling his eyes. I thought either he was going to have a seizure or dive on me again when he suddenly flipped over, held his decently sized prick in his hand, and put his other hand on the back of my neck drawing me to him.

"Where are we?"

I was on. "We're in the men's john at Times Square in the subway."

"No, no," he shrieked. "We're in the ladies room at the Four Seasons and you're admiring my voluptuous breasts."

"Goodbye, Paul."

I didn't break off with Polina right away. I guess
I needed her too much—the conversations, the
theater, and her stories of Europe where she grew
up. I tried to ignore the sex, but Polina was getting more and more into it. It hit rock bottom for
me when she wanted to be told she was a golden
shower queen. Polina had saved her urine in
empty glass Macademia nut jars for me to admire
while I told her the story of her mighty pissing
powers in yet another fantasy men's john. No
way I could hack that. I asked her if maybe we
could be friends and she nearly had a coronary.

"Friends, what do you mean, friends? Here I
am on the threshold of powerful sexual discoveries
and you want to be friends?"

I tried to tell her to find other women, but she
wanted me. She wanted me but she was ashamed
of me. She wouldn't introduce me to her friends or

let me come by for her at work. Afraid I'd flash a lavender neon "L" between my tits, I suppose. More out of loneliness than love I stayed with her. My classes at school were all men and they had it in for me since I was doing better than they were. Of all careers I thought film would be somewhat open, but their pathetic egos had bloated to outrageous proportions behind a small Arriflex and they resented a woman who could compete on "their" territory and worse, win. The bars weren't a hotbed of intellectual ferment, even though I had found some nice ones uptown where the merest hint of roles would have frozen you out. Roles were for truck drivers to these women. But I could only take so many conversations where big names were dropped like napalm to inflame your brain with admiration. I don't give a shit who you know, I care about what you do. These high-class dollies weren't doing much. But I couldn't go back to the sleazy Colony or Sugar's where the bulls still put butch hair wax on their crew cuts. So there was Polina for all her fantasies, a seemingly better choice than any of the others.

It was Alice who resolved the problem. The three of us would go out from time to time. I was too dangerous for her friends but I was good enough for her daughter. Polina's double-think was astounding. She encouraged my bond with Alice. We were closer in age than Polina and I were, which wouldn't have made a difference if Polina didn't harp about her age constantly. Alice was only six years younger than I was. I began to feel guilty for being born in 1944. The "old lady," as she referred to herself, looked down her nose at our music, the films we shared, and the magazines we read. She was not above patronizing either one of us for our years and our tastes which drew Alice and I closer together, as generational hostility always does. Alice knew her mother and I were lovers and she thought it was great. She also knew about Paul and considered him the original human slug. One yellow, acid drizzle day she confessed, "You know Mom wants to sleep with me?"

"Oh yeah?"

"She won't admit it but I know she does. I think I'd like to sleep with her. She's very good looking, you know. Too bad it would freak her out. Incest doesn't seem like such a trauma to me."

"Me neither, but then I can't really say much about that because I didn't grow up with my real parents. But I never have been able to figure out why parents and children put each other in these desexed categories. It's antihuman, I think."

"Yeah, parents get freaked out about everything. Mom must have a heavy case of repression going, because she'll never deal with the fact that she digs my body."

"She's got more going than that."

"Oh yeah? What's the old girl cooking up?"

"Nothing. Just don't sleep with your mother. I'm not against incest if both parties consent and are over fifteen, but your mother's on her own weird trip."

"Tell me her trip."

"No, I don't kiss and tell."

"Oh Molly, why do you have to have morals?"

"Because I don't have money."

"How are your morals when it comes to sleeping with me? I'm jail bait, ya know."

"Alice, your spirit of romance is so delicate. Moves me to tears."

"Please sleep with me. I feel like I can trust you. You won't get into a big, heavy thing about it, you know?"

"I know, but what about your mother?"

"What she doesn't know won't hurt her." Alice giggled and slipped me a sly look. "I'll give you one perfect, yellow rose for your sunshine soul and then will you sleep with me?"

"For one perfect yellow rose—yes."

Alice jogged down Broadway looking for a florist's shop, ran inside a tiny one, and emerged, rose in hand. Off we went to 17th Street, to the cockroaches and the steam heat that never steamed. But Alice steamed and shook and sighed, and she hadn't one sexual quirk in her mind. She loved being touched and she loved touching back. Kissing was an art form to her. She was there, all there with no hang-ups, no stories to tell, just herself. And I was just me.

Alice's survival instincts were sound. She knew we'd have to sneak around to see each other more often. Polina's warped Victorian mentality would get watersoaked if she read our beads. When the three of us were out together, it was a unique form of torture. Once in the balcony watching *Rozencrantz and Gildenstern Are Dead*, Polina held my left hand while Alice played with my right thigh. The play made no impression on me at all, but I clapped wildly at the end to let off all that trapped energy.

Polina threw us together, hoping it would happen, yet terrified of it at the same time. Somehow

I was the sexual go-between for both of them. I was a kind of telestar for them to bounce messages off to each other. There were times when I felt lonelier with them than without them.

One Saturday afternoon looking out over Harlem and hearing the steady drums from the park, mother and daughter entered a time-honored fight. Polina accused Alice of behaving like a child over some trivial item and Alice replied that Polina was suffering from hardening of the arteries, specifically in her head. This kind of cheerful banter went on until Alice in a fit of untried ego hit her oldest competitor: "I'm not a baby anymore. For Christ's sake, Mother, I'm old enough to be making it with your lover, so dig it and get off my back."

"My what?"

"Molly and I are lovers."

Polina recoiled. She fumed in Italian and rattled so fast all I could catch was "Basta! Basta!" and a slap across the face. When her streak of bilingualism petered out she ordered me out of her life and Alice's life forever in unmistakable English. Alice protested, but Polina curbed that strike with the threat that she wouldn't send Alice to college if Alice persisted in this relationship. Alice was a shrewd sort and she had no intention of working her way through college, especially after contact with my life. She bowed to her mother's superior material force. And I gracefully exited to 17th Street where the hounds of hell gnawed at my ankles and the waterbugs organized a safari through my kitchen.

I dreamed of sewer lagoons underneath the skyscrapers, where I could navigate a Con Edison

raft to take me out of this crazy city with its crazy
people. Give me one sharp pole to fight off the
blind alligators thrown into the drainpipes by
people who bought them as babies on trips to
Miami Beach. Miami Beach, so close to Carrie
with her crotons, ixora, and blind pride. Miami
Beach where the geriatric generation buys se-
quined colostemy bags to match their shoes. Even
if I made it through the drainpipes to the Inter-
coastal I couldn't land there. There is no place to
go. Here I am in the Hanging Gardens of Neon,
hustling my ass for a degree and living in shit.
Shit worse than Shiloh and damn, is there one
person in Manhattan who isn't a radiated disaster
area? Maybe it's me. Maybe I'm the disaster area,
or am I still full of Dunkard ways and simple
dreams? Maybe I belong in the foothills of Pennsylvania with the Mennonites and the Amish and
how the hell can I make movies out there? You
can't even have electric light bulbs out there. In
Logic 101 this is called being on the horns of a
dilemma. Either way you get gored. But if I had
money maybe I could slip out of that dilemma.
I mean, if I had money I wouldn't be at the mercy
of chance, peanut intellects, and amputated emo-
tions so much. With money you can protect
yourself. But getting it is another story. One more
year and I'll be out of school. An instant fortune.
Oh sure, I can slip into the cracks of the pavement,
because no one will hire me. Shit. Well, I'm not
giving up. But I'd like to rest every now and then.
I'd like to see the hills of Shiloh again and lay my
body down in the meadow behind Ep's place, out
where they buried Jenna. Maybe the smell of the

clover will get me through one more winter in this branch of hell. Maybe I can keep myself together with a day in the country. There's still no price on the sun.

I hit the road and hitched to Philadelphia. There I got picked up by a truck driver of the male variety who tried to feel me up when I fell asleep, but I snarled at him and he withdrew his offending paw. He dropped me off at the bus station in Lancaster. After an hour's wait in the hazy lethargy of the Greyhound terminal I boarded the bus. With a rumble it roared off farting thick black pollution in its wake, fouling the low green hills of southeastern Pennsylvania. The hills were also fouled with huge billboards advertising Tanya and Ford and saying "Drink milk, it's nature's perfect food." Every now and then I could catch a glimpse of the countryside through the thickets of advertising.

Once in York, I had to catch two buses, but I finally got to Shiloh. The green bus stopped in front of Mrs. Hershener's and I jumped out. Same old screen door, same tarpaper shavings in the drive. The porch was half decayed and the Nehi sign had been changed to 7-Up the Uncola but those were the only signs of fifteen years of progress. The road down to Ep's place was still dirt with a few blue stones thrown on it to pretend it would be serviceable in the rains. The sun was high over my head and milk-white butterflies chased butter-yellow ones over June grass and plowed earth. I took a deep breath of air and got higher than orange sunshine could ever get me.

My feet took off and carried my body down the road. I was running and pumping and pushing those legs that damn near had shin splints from all that New York City pavement. Pretty soon I was waving my arms and yelling and there wasn't one face to look at me and think, "What's that nut doing?" There was nobody in sight, just the butterflies.

Around the bend, down the hill, and there was the old frame house. Wash was on the line and the house had a fresh coat of white paint. I went up to the door, out of breath, and knocked, but no one was home. Good, because I didn't feel like asking anybody if I could go rest by their pond. In the little patch of concrete by the front porch were the two pennies stuck in there when Leroy and I started first grade. "Long as we got those two cents," Carrie would say, "we ain't broke." The rabbit pens were gone and the pig wallow had been planted with pansies and fandango petunias.

The pond was the same old pond. The edge was rimmed with green slime and tall grass full of frogs' eggs jutted from the still water. Foam gathered around the tall grass. I dropped down by the pool, put my arms behind my head and watched the clouds. After awhile the insects and birds took me for a rock. A caterpillar bumped across my left elbow and a mockingbird was careful to shit on my foot.

I opened my eyes, slowly turned my head, and stared straight into the eyes of the biggest goddamn frog I'd ever seen. That frog wasn't scared of me, that frog was defiant. It stared at me, blinked then puffed up a red-pink throat and let out a croak that would have delivered Jericho. From the other side of the pond came a returning belch. And two little green heads peeked out of the water to investigate this mammal on the shore. Amphibians must think we're inferior creatures since we can't go in and out of the water the way they can. Besides being biologically superior, that ole frog is more together than I am. That frog doesn't want to make movies. That frog hasn't even seen movies and furthermore that frog doesn't give a big damn. It just swims, eats, makes love, and sings as it pleases. Whoever heard of a neurotic frog? Where do humans get off thinking they're the pinnacle of evolution?

As if to let me know what it thought of my cognitive processes, the Goliath let out a mighty bellow and flew straight up in the air, terrifying a dragonfly cruising at low altitude. Its four feet touched earth; it hurled itself back into the air and landed in the pond with a truly heroic splash that soaked half my shirt. I sat up and watched the ripples race each other to the edge, where they were lost in the scum; then I saw its huge head pop up out of the weeds. That damn frog winked at me.

I got up, brushed myself off, and trotted down by the gully, through the drainpipe and out the other side and started up the road to Leota's old house. I congratulated myself on being small enough and skinny enough to slip through the drainpipe.

Mrs. Bisland was still living in that house. The shrubs had grown and it had aluminum siding but other than that, it looked the same. She looked pretty much the same too except now she was completely gray. She was surprised to see me, fussed over me, and asked how Carrie was and how sorry she was to hear about Carl passing on back there in '61. Did I know Leota had married Jackie Phantom, who owns a body shop right out in West York, and they're doing real good? She gave me their address on Diamond Street and I trudged back to Mrs. Hershener's, went in, and bought a raspberry ice cream cone. The lady behind the counter told me Mrs. Hershener hung herself three years ago and not a soul knew why.

Mrs. Bisland called Leota because she was looking for me. I didn't have time to knock on the door before it opened and there was Leota—same cat eyes, same languid body, but oh god, she looked forty-five years old and she had two brats hanging on her like possums. I looked twenty-four. She saw herself in my reflection and there was a flicker of pain in her eyes.

"Molly, come in. This is Jackie, Jr. and this is Margie, named for my mother. Say hello to the lady."

Jackie, Jr. at five could say hello with a reasonable degree of accuracy but Margie hung back. I think she'd never seen a woman in pants before.

"Hello, Margie. Hello, Jackie."

"Now Jackie take your sister out in the back and play."

"I don't wanna take her out and play. I wanna stay here with you."

"Do as you're told."

"No." He pouted until he near tripped over his lip.

Leota slapped him one on the back, collared

him out the door, and the screams didn't die down for twenty minutes.

"They drive me crazy sometimes but I love them."

"Sure," I said. What else could I say? Every mother says the same thing.

"What brings you to York?"

"Thought I'd take a day out of the big city."

"Big city? You aren't in Florida? Oh, that's right. I believe I did hear from Mother that you'd gone up to New York. Aren't you afraid you'll get killed in the streets—all them Puerto Ricans and niggers?"

"No." There was an awkward silence.

"Not that whites can't be violent too. But you're up there where all kinds of people are bunched together. I'm not prejudiced, you understand."

"I understand."

"Are you married yet?"

"Don't you remember? I told you when we were kids that I was never getting married. I kept my promise."

"Oh, you just haven't met the right man." Nervous laugh.

"Right. Everybody says that but it's a load of shit."

Her face registered the obscenity but a faint hint of admiration played at the corners of her mouth. "I married Jack right out of high school. I wanted to get out of the house and that was the only way, but I loved him too. He's a good husband. Works hard, loves the kids. I couldn't ask for more. You should see Carol Morgan. She married Eddie Harper, remember him? He was two years ahead of us—he drinks himself sick. I was lucky."

I looked at the neat little house with plastic covers on the furniture and ceramic lamps. The kitchen had a table top full of kidney shapes in thin lines over the formica and there was a bunch of plastic mums as a centerpiece. The living room was an oasis of avocado wall-to-wall carpeting. Leota would have shuddered to see my milk cartons.

Jackie, Jr. either shut up or developed an early case of throat cancer, because at last we could lower our voices.

"Would you like coffee or soda or something?"

"Coke."

She went into the kitchen and pulled out of an enormous decorator-brown refrigerator a 16 oz. coke. As she walked back to hand it to me, I noticed her body had lost its coiled suppleness and she dragged a bit; her breasts sagged and her hair was dull.

"What are you doing up there in the big city?"

"Finishing up at N.Y.U. I'm in filmmaking."

She was so impressed. "Are you going to be a movie star? You look a little like Natalie Wood, you know."

"Thank you for the compliment, but I don't think I'm movie star material. I want to make the movies, not be one of the pawns in them."

"Oh"—she couldn't say any more because it was a mysterious process and all she saw in the end were the movie stars anyway.

"Leota, have you ever thought about that night we spent together?"

Her back stiffened and her eyes receded. "No, never."

"Sometimes I do. We were so young and I think we must have been kind of sweet."

"I don't think about those kinds of things. I'm a mother."

"What does that do, shut down the part of your brain that remembers the past?"

"I'm too busy for that stuff. Who has time to think? Anyway, that was perverted, sick. I haven't got time for it."

"I'm sorry to hear that."

"Why did you ask me that? Why'd you come back here—to ask me that? You must have stayed that way. Is that why you're walking around in jeans and a pullover? You one of those sickies? I don't understand it. I don't understand it at all, a pretty girl like you. You could have lots of men. You have more choices than I did here in this place."

"I thought you said you liked your husband."

"I love my husband. Love my children. That's what a woman is made for. It's just you living in a big city and being educated—you could marry a doctor or a lawyer or even someone in t.v."

"Leota, I will never marry."

"You're crazy. A woman's got to marry. What's going to happen to you when you're fifty? You got to grow old with somebody. You're going to be sorry."

"I'm going to be arrested for throwing an orgy at ninety-nine and I'm not growing old with anybody. What a gruesome thought. Christ, you're twenty-four and you're worried about being fifty. That makes no sense."

"Makes all the sense in the world. I have to

think about security. I have to save our money and plan ahead for the children's educations and our retirement. I didn't get an education and I want to be sure the kids get them."

"You could go to school if you wanted to—there are community colleges and all that."

"I'm too old. Got too much to do. I don't think I can sit in a classroom and learn any more. It's fine that you're doing it, I admire you for it. You can meet a lot of people that way and someday you'll meet the right one and settle down. You just wait."

"Let's stop this shit. I love women. I'll never marry a man and I'll never marry a woman either. That's not my way. I'm a devil-may-care lesbian."

Leota took her breath in sharply. "You ought to have your head examined, girl. They put people like you away. You need help."

"Yes, I know people like you who put people like me away. Before you call down the acolytes of Heterosexual Inquisition, I'm splitting."

"Don't go using those big words on me, Molly Bolt. You always were a smartass."

"Yeah—and I was your first lover, too." I slammed the door and was down the street by the used car lot. She could have died on the spot for all I know.

Now to retrace my steps to Babylon on the Hudson. Back to the place where the air destroys your lungs and the footfall behind you might belong to the hand that slits your throat. Back to where glitzy Broadway hosts the suburbs nightly and calls it the theater. Back to where slick glossies pounce on flesh and serve it up monthly to the nation's subscription cannibals. Back to where millions of us live side by side in rotting honeycombs and never say hello. Polluted, packed, putrid, it's the only place where I have any room, any hope. I got to go back and stick it out. At least in New York City I can be more than a breeder of the next generation.

New York City didn't greet me with open arms on
my return but that didn't matter. I was determined
to deal with all eventualities, even indifference.
The remainder of the summer droned on. Fall
came as a relief because it would be my senior
year and in our senior year we were expected to
produce a short film, an accumulation of all our
years of study at N.Y.U.

Professor Walgren, head of the department and
dedicated misogynist, called me in his office for
the routine consideration of a project.

"Molly, what are you going to do for your senior
project?"

"I thought I'd do a twenty-minute documentary
of one woman's life." He seemed unimpressed.
Pornoviolence was in this year and all the men
were busy shooting bizarre fuck scenes with cuts

of pigs beating up people at the Chicago convention spliced between the sexual encounters. My project was not in that vein.

"You might have trouble getting the camera out for weekends. By the way, who will be in your crew?"

"No one. No one will consent to be my crew."

Prof. Walgren coughed behind his fashionable wire-rim glasses and said with a slight hint of malice, "Oh, I see, they won't take orders from a woman, eh?"

"I don't know. I hadn't noticed they were too good at taking orders from each other."

"Well, good luck on your film. I'll be eager to see what you crank out."

Sure you will, you fake-hippie, middle-aged washout.

The cameras were booked for the next decade but that always happened whenever I asked to use one out of the studio. So that afternoon I casually dumped the Arriflex into a tubby wicker tote bag with Jamaica sewn across its side in multicolored thread and waltzed out. I had also ripped off as much film as I could carry in the bag and the special inside pockets I had sewn in my pea coat. I went home and asked my neighbor to water my plants for the next week, gave her the extra key, and went up to Port Authority—home of the nation's tearoom queens—where I caught a bus for Ft. Lauderdale. Thirty-four hours and five grilling conversations later I was behind the Howard Johnson's on Route One. The sun was so bright after New York that everything seemed harsh to me and my eyes hurt. The equipment was too heavy for me to carry the four miles home so I hired a taxi.

Ten minutes later we were zipping up Flagler Drive by the Florida East Coast Railway, next to the house. The pink had faded from flaming ugly to mild grotesque. The queen palm in the front lawn had grown at least fifteen feet and all the shrubs around the house were busy with flowers and chameleons. I hadn't been home in six years. I wrote Carrie once or twice to tell her I was still alive but that was about it. I didn't tell her I was coming home to see her.

I knocked on the door and heard a slow shuffle behind the half-opened jalousies. The jalousies were turned open and a scratchy voice said, "Who is it?"

"It's me, Mom. It's Molly."

"Molly!" The door flew open and I saw Carrie. She looked like a yellow prune and her hair was stark white. Her hands shook as she reached out to bring me closer and give me a hug. She started to cry and she couldn't talk very well, her tongue seemed heavy in her mouth. She swayed from side to side as she tried to walk back into the living room. I put my hand under her elbow and guided her to her old rocker with the swan's heads for armrests. She sat down and looked at me.

"I guess you're surprised to see your old mother after all these years. My sickness caught up with me. I'm drying up like grass in the drought."

"I'm sorry, Mom. I didn't know anything about it."

"No, and I didn't want you to know nothin' about it neither. After you left, I decided to keep things to myself. You didn't care, anyway. I told Florence never to write and tell you about my condition. I can hardly write anymore 'cause it's got my fingers too. What are you doing here? You're not living under this roof and laying back there in that bedroom with naked women. I hope you know that."

"I know that. I came back to ask you to help me with my senior project."

"Not if it costs money, I ain't."

"It doesn't cost anything."

"And what are you doing in school? You should have graduated in 1967. You're two years behind time. What, those Yankee kids too smart for you?"

"No, I had to work full time most of the last three years and it slowed me down in school."

"Ha, good. I'm glad to hear those snotty-nosed, Jew-brats up there ain't smarter than you."

"Well, will you help me with my project?"

"No, I don't know what it is yet. What do I hafta do?"

"All you have to do is sit in that rocker and talk to me while I film you."

"Film me!"

"Sure."

"You mean I'm gonna be in a movie?"

"Right."

"But I got no clothes, no make up. You got to be decked out for something like that. I'm too old to be in a movie."

"Just sit in your chair and wear your housedress with the black poodles on it. That's all you have to do."

"What am I going to say? You writ some play for me to make a fool outa myself in? You used

225

to write things like that when you was little. I ain't doing no play, you put that in your pipe and smoke it."

"No play, Mom. All I want you to do is to talk to me while I film you. Like we're doing now."

"Well now, I think I can do that."

"Good, then you'll do it?"

"No, not until I know what you're gonna do with it."

"It's my senior project. I need it to graduate. I'll show it to my professors."

"Oh no. I ain't talking for no professors so's they can laugh at my English. Nothing doing."

"No one will laugh unless you say something funny. Come on, please. It's not such a big thing to sit there and talk."

"If you promise not to make a fool outa me, then I'll do it. And you have to buy your food while you're here because I ain't got the money to feed you."

"That's okay. I brought along enough money for a week."

"All right then. Go put your stuff in the back room but mind, no women are coming to this house while you're in it—not even the Avon lady. You hear me?"

"I hear you. Hey, where's ole Florence?"

"Florence died a year ago last May. High blood pressure's what did it. Doctor gave it a fancy name but it was high blood pressure just the same. Her being so nervous, all the time worrying about other people's business. Poking her nose where it don't belong. That kind of carrying on will kill you. But she was a good sister and I miss her."

The Mouth dead. It seemed impossible. Even

dead she must be babbling in her grave. Carrie continued, "We buried her in the same lot as Carl. You remember, over there by the drive-in theater? Oh, it was a lovely ceremony. Only thing that spoiled it was the advertisement for the movie —some sex film, something like *Hot Flesh Pots*. Well, it was a good thing Florence was dead because if she had seen that it would have killed her. She must have been turning over in her casket. You shoulda seen the casket. Shiny black, next to the most expensive kind. You know how she hated suggestive things. They could have taken that nasty sign down when they saw her shiny casket coming down the road. This time I rode in a black Cadillac. Wasn't as nice as the car we rode in for Carl's funeral. What kind of car was that?"

"A Continental."

"Let me tell you that Cadillac got nothin' on those Continentals. If I'm ever a rich woman I'm getting a Continental. Who makes them?"

"Ford."

"Ford. Your father told me never to buy a Ford motor car. Said they were made outa cardboard and he knew what he was talking about. But I still think a Continental has a smooth ride."

"Daddy probably never rode in one so use your own judgment when you make your millions."

Carrie cackled and flicked her wrist at me. "Go on, put that junk back in your room before I trip over it and break my neck."

I picked up the equipment and carried it down the terrazzo halls to the back room that used to be mine. Carrie had taken all my ribbons and trophies off the walls and put up a picture facing the double bed. It was Christ kneeling at Gethsem-

ane with a ray of heavenly light coming out of the
night to hit him full in the bearded face. Over the
head of the brown-painted, iron bedstead she had
an enormous dayglo cross. On the sagging dresser
stood a ceramic chipmunk wearing a University
of Florida freshman beanie. I deposited the stuff in
the closet and went into the front room.

Carrie was pushing herself in the rocker with
one of her feet and getting very animated. "You
want a cup of tea, honey? How about a coke? I
always keep coke in the refrigerator. Leroy's little
boys like it so much. You should see them. Ep
the second is five and a half years old. Leroy got
the girl pregnant, that's why he's so old, if you
know what I mean. Leroy married her in the nick
of time. But they seem happy. Accidents will
happen. Look at you. Ha! Maybe they'll come by
sometime this week and you can see them. I don't
get out much any more other than what they take
me. Lost the car. Had to sell it when the city put
main sewage pipes in. Didn't have money so I
sold the car to pay for the price of having the yard
dug up so I could connect. Damn crooks. City,
state, president, they're all damn crooks. Terrible
to be without a car but I'm too old to drive I guess.
My illness, you know. Can't get my hands and
feets to do right together. Leroy said it was the
best thing that I sold the old Plymouth. Said he
was afraid I'd get myself killed on the highway.
So now I go out in the backyard but I miss driving
up by the beach. Leroy takes me up with the kids
now and then. Kids make too much noise. I don't
remember you making all that noise. You were
a quiet child. Did you tell me how long you're
gonna be here?"

"Around a week, if it's okay."

"That's fine so long as you buy your own food. Meat prices are fierce these days. I only eat meat once or twice a week now. Not like when we lived in Shiloh and got fresh meat whenever we wanted it. For the killing. I don't see how people with big families live."

"How are you living? You don't look like you can work."

"Oh yes I can. I certainly can. I take in ironing and I sit down so it don't tax me so much. I ain't on handouts. I get forty-five dollars from social security and since I'm over sixty-five I get Medicare but that's no handout. I earned that. I paid years of taxes so those things belong to me. When I get too old or too sick to work I'm walking over to the ocean to let the fishes eat me. You don't have to worry about taking care of me, girl."

"I'm not worried."

"See, you don't care. You don't even write me when you're away. I could die down here and you wouldn't even know it. You don't care."

"Mom, when I left I understood that you didn't want any more to do with me. Besides, I did write once in awhile."

"Angry words, angry words. You should know a mother don't mean angry words to her child."

"You said I wasn't your child and you were glad of it."

"Oh no, I didn't. I never said such a thing."

"Mom, you did."

"Don't go telling me what I did. You misunderstood me. You're a little hothead. You flew outa here before I could talk to you. I never said no such thing and don't you try to tell me I did.

You're my baby. Why in 1944, when I was worrying over whether to adopt you, Pastor Needle, you remember, our old pastor up north, he told me you were born to be my baby and that all children come into this world the same way and I wasn't to worry about you being a bastard. No sir, all children are the same in the eyes of the Lord. I don't know where you get such ideas in your head. You know I'd never say a thing like that. Why I love you. You're all I got left in this world."

"Yeah, okay, Mom."

I went out in the kitchen and got a soda and some big, hard pretzels out of the breadbox. Carrie wanted some but she had to soak them in her coffee because her teeth were going bad. We sat in the living room with the t.v. turned on full blast and talked during commercials in the Lawrence Welk show. She told me how she thought Lawrence Welk was a wonderful man and his show was wholesome. She wanted to dance to all that beautiful music, but she'd fall over because her inside ear was out of whack.

I filmed Carrie through the week. Once over her initial fright she relaxed in her rocker and talked a blue streak. Whenever she'd get excited about anything she'd start pushing the rocker harder and harder until she'd be whizzing away and running her mouth as fast as the chair. Then when she'd finished her story she'd let the rocker coast back to idle and she'd answer questions with a *yes* or a *no*. She thoroughly enjoyed the attention and she was thrilled that I could work a camera. It didn't take her long to figure things out because when I took a shot of her revving up her rocker she snapped, "What are you doing taking pictures of my feet? People wanna see my face not my feet."

When I wasn't filming I did household chores for her—cut the grass and ran errands since she couldn't walk anywhere. And Leroy did come over with his wife and kids. He and Mom talked about little things while the kids ran through the house and Leroy's wife, Joyce, eyed me uncomfortably. She had her hair in a teased beehive and her makeup preceded her in the room by three inches. She was afraid Leroy would find me attractive. Nervously she told me, "Why you look like one of those models in *Mademoiselle* magazine with your hair and wearing pants and love beads. You must be a real hippie."

"No, I looked like this before it became fashionable. Poverty's a great trend setter these days."

"Yeah, my tomboy, Molly, she looks real good now. I knew you'd turn out all right," Carrie boasted. My looks were still more important to Carrie than anything I would ever achieve. "You'd look like a real lady if you'd get outa them jeans," she fussed.

"Oh but that's the rage now," Joyce fumbled.

Leroy added in his butchest voice, "Yeah, the women want to wear the pants nowadays so I tell my wife to go on out and support me, I'll take care of the kids."

Carrie laughed and Leroy's wife snapped at his elbow, "Leroy, shut up."

Carrie dragged Joyce loaded with hair spray back into her bedroom to look at a housedress she had sewn on her old White Rose machine with the treadle. Leroy turned to me, "We sure grew up, didn't we?"

"It happens to the best of us."

"And you're making movies. I never thought you'd make movies. I thought you was gonna be a lawyer with that mouth of yours. You always were smarter than forty crickets. I guess I'm dumb. After the Marine Corps I came on back here and got a job working for a lawn care operation. I like being outside. Always did."

"I remember that."

"Yeah, I got four men working under me too. Coloreds. They're just like us. I mean I wouldn't socialize with 'em but the guys on the work gang, they're just like me. Got wives and kids and car payments. We get on fine. I learned that in the service. Had to learn there. It was good for me. Ep filled me with all kinds of crap and the service kicked it outa me for sure. I went to Nam. Did you know that?"

"No, I didn't even know you were in the service."

"Marines, not just the service. Yeah, yeah I went over there and got a good look at the gooks. I started out as a diesel mechanic. Always was good with machines, you remember."

"I remember the time you took the Bonneville apart and lost your clutch cable."

"That was a beautiful bike. I'd like to get another one but Joyce is scared to death of them. Still like tooling with machines. I went into diesels because I didn't want to get shot at. Got shot at anyway. God, I was glad to get back from there."

"Did you kill anyone?"

"I don't know. I shot at anything that moved but I never heard a yell so maybe I didn't. I only got shot at a couple of times, it's not like I was out there in the rice paddies. You can't see anything anyway but you sure can smell it when it's been dead for a couple days."

"Well, I'm glad you're back in one piece, Leroy."

"Yeah, me too. It's a shitass war. Hey, you got a boyfriend?"

"Why the hell are you asking me that? No, I haven't got a boyfriend."

"But you been with men. I mean, you been with other men than me?" His voice was low.

"Of course. Why?"

"I dunno. I just wondered. You're still the only girl I can talk to."

"Except I'm a woman now, Leroy, with a capital *W*."

He looked at me, puzzled. "I can see that. You look good, Molly, real good."

"Thanks."

"You ever go with girls?"

"What the hell is this, twenty questions?"

"Uh, well, I haven't seen you in so long. I just wondered, you know."

"I know. I go out with girls every chance I get. How do you like them apples, toots?"

He studied me and then with a resigned sigh: "It's just as well. You ain't the kind to settle down. You always said that but I didn't listen to you." He hesitated, then leaned forward, lowering his voice to a whisper. "It gets boring, you know? I think somedays I'm gonna walk off the job and go down to Bahia Mar and get me a job as a crew member on a fat private yacht and sail around the world. Maybe someday I'll do that."

"If you do, make sure you leave your family enough to live on."

At that instant the happy brood reappeared.

"Your Aunt Carrie's got some new housedresses, Leroy. One's a pretty orange like the color I wanted for my new shoes."

Leroy looked helpless. "That's nice, honey."

"We have to get these wild Indians to bed. Come on, hon, and say goodbye to your cousin. Aunt Carrie, we'll see you next week. Let's all drive out and see the new condominiums they built up above Galt Ocean Mile."

With a look of desperation, Leroy shook my hand. Then he cautiously put his left hand on my right shoulder and gave me a quick kiss on the cheek. He didn't look into my eyes but turned his head and said to Carrie, "We won't see her for another five years, huh, 'Mom?'"

Carrie bellowed, "You'll see her before then if I croak."

"Aunt Carrie, don't say such things," Joyce gently urged.

"You take care, Molly, and let us hear from you every now and then."

"Sure, Leroy, take care of your own self."

He backed out the front door and got into a worn white station wagon, turned the ignition, switched on the lights, and honked the horn when he got out on the road.

"Don't he have a lovely family and his wife is so sweet? I love that Joyce."

"Yeah, they're nice, real nice."

The day that I was to leave to go home, Carrie acted like her old self. Somehow she pushed her wasting body through the kitchen like a whirlwind. She insisted on making me fried eggs and fresh-brewed coffee. Carrie considered instant coffee a sign of moral degeneracy and she was bound to make me fresh coffee even if it killed her.

After all this activity she sat down at the kitchen table, stammered, then began: "You always asked me who your real father was. I never told you. You're such a nosy bastard you'll find out after I'm dead so I might as well tell you myself so I know you'll get the story straight. Ruby had taken up with some foreigner and worse, he was married. That's why it all got hushed up."

"What kind of foreigner was he?"

"French, full-blooded French and them's the rottenest set. They're even crazier than Wops. We all nearly died when we found out she was running with him and he couldn't hardly speak English. How they talked to each other is beyond me. Probably for what they were doing they didn't need no talking. Ruby had hot pants. Anyway, when he found out she was pregnant he jilted her. Carl tracked him down and made him agree to never claim you, to stay out of your life and Ruby's. He was happy to agree to that."

"Did you ever see him?"

"No, but they say he was a handsome devil. That's where you got sharp features and dark eyes. You don't look a whit like Ruby except you got her voice, exactly. Whenever I hear you talk if I close my eyes I can see Ruby standing there. You ain't built like her, nothing like her 'cept that voice. You must be your old man all over. And you talk with your hands and French people do that. He was a big athlete, you know. Oh yes, well known he was, in the Olympics or something. God knows where she met him. Ruby never went near a playing field in her life. Bet that's where you got all your coordination, from him. She was a clumsy ass."

"What was his name?"

"One of those damn French names, two names strung together. I can't pronounce it. Something like John-Peter Bullette."

"Jean-Pierre?"

"That's it. Why the hell those people got to name themselves twice. Because they like themselves so much I suppose, the more names they got the longer it takes you to get it out of your mouth. None of our family's like that, dreamy like those French. That's where you get all your dreaminess and being an artist. We're practical people. We were always practical people and we eat sensible food too. Those Frogs eat snails. Not only do they eat them, they charge you an arm and a leg for them. Never heard of anything so damn dumb in all my life."

"I'm glad you told me, Mom. I used to wonder about it a lot."

"I ain't done telling you. Don't try to cut me off. I've been holding this in since before you were born and now that I'm near the grave I'm getting it off my chest." She looked down at her wrinkled chest and hooted, "I ain't got no chest to get it off of. You know, when I was young I had pretty tits, just like a model for a brassiere ad. This dern disease dries everything up. Gettin' old is terrible. Just wait, you'll find out. Here I look down and see nothing but a sugar cake with a raisin on it when I used to look down and see two full oranges." She put her hand under her breast and pushed it up. "Hell, that don't even do no good."

"You want another cup of coffee, Mom?"

"Believe I will. There's more milk in the refrigerator if you'll get it for me. Milk cost nearly as much as whiskey. I might as well go out and spend the money on whiskey and pour that in my coffee. It'd make me feel better. We couldn't have children. Now that's a whole damn sorry story and I'm gonna tell you the whole thing so's you don't get it from the wrong people when I'm gone. Carl got syphilis the first time he had a piece of ass back in 1919. That I adjusted to when I found out, but then in 1937 I found out he was cheatin' on me, yes, cheatin'. I didn't say a thing about it. Everybody knew but me. Cookie, Florence, Joe—they'd all seen him at the movies with her but they never told me. Only time in her life that Florence kept her mouth shut. Coulda wrung her neck for it. The wife is always the last to know. I'd have never guessed it. He didn't seem any different to me. Treated me like always, bought me little presents. You know how he was that way. He acted like he loved me. Then we went to a party at the Detweilers and everyone was whispering. I thought they were all talking about me so I said, 'What goes here? Are you all talking about me?' Florence said, 'Somebody should tell her.' Now I was worried for sure and I said, 'Just what the hell is going on?' Everybody clammed up and Cookie hustled Florence into the kitchen. Carl and I went home. I knew something was up. The next day old Pop-pop came down all the way from Hanover to tell me. The gang all decided he should be the one to do it, after all he was my stepfather and the only relative I had left aside from Florence. Pop-pop told me that my Carl was seeing a woman named Gladys and she looked very tall and elegant. I couldn't believe it, not after what happened with my first husband."

"Your first husband. I didn't know you had any husband other than Carl."

"Oh yes, I was married once before, right before I'd'a gone to high school in 1918. Rup was his name and he beat tar outa me so I divorced him. And he ran with other women too. It was a scandal that I divorced him. People thought that was worse than him running with women. Those days you didn't get divorced. That's when I started smoking too. Goddamn, they think I'm trash for getting a divorce I'll just smoke on the streets and really give them something to chew over. I smoked big cigars too so's nobody could miss it." She paused and picked up the thread of her original thought. "When Carl came home that night I knew I'd have to dope it out with him. I asked him what was this about him and Gladys. He told me the truth. Been seeing her for a year, he said. And he sat on that old sofa we had with the brown stripes, put his head in his hands and cried. Tears running down his face and he says to me, 'Cat, can't you love more than one person at a time? I love two people. What can I do?' I lost my mind then. How could he love anyone but me? If he couldn't be satisfied with me I was packing my bags and getting out. I loved that man. I worshipped him. He was so good to me how could he turn around and do that? I almost landed in the nut house in Harrisburg and right after my cobalt treatments. I wasn't right in the head from that yet. I got on the bus once to go to downtown York and ended up in Spring Grove. I didn't know east from west. Well, I carried on high and cried so much they took me to Dr. Harmeling because they thought I was losing my sight. Then Doc had a conference with Carl and me. Doc told Carl he was crazy to be with another woman. One was enough, was his thought. Put a paper bag over their head and women are all the same. Why couldn't Carl be happy with the one he's got? I was right in the room when the doctor said that. At least Doc was on my side. I was a good wife. So Carl broke off with that woman and I forgave him. But he broke my heart. I could never forget it. To this day I can't believe he did that to me." Her voice trailed off into a whine. She wiped the tears from her eyes with a napkin and looked down in her coffee cup, waiting for me to sympathize with her.

Thirty-one years ago and her life froze in that year. She enameled the sharp edge of misery into a pearl of passion. Her life revolved around that emotional peak since the day she discovered it and now she was waiting for me to share it. "I'm sorry, Mom, but, well, it doesn't make sense to me to stay with only one person either."

Her head jerked up and she glared at me. "Such talk. You're oversexed, that's what's wrong with you."

I looked at her blankly. I wasn't going to encourage her in her ridiculous triumph that she was the most wronged woman in the hemisphere.

She took a breath and continued with less conviction and emotion since I wasn't supporting her. "Then in '44 you were born. I saw my chance. He couldn't give me no baby so I went after you. I always wanted a baby to dress and care for. I thought you would make me happy. I sewed clothes for you, took you out in a carriage. You were a beautiful baby once we put some meat on your bare little bones. They weren't feeding you in that Catholic orphanage. Nuns—never liked them anyway. They look like penguins to me. Carl was afraid he'd be an unfit father but he said he'd try to do right. He grew to love you. Loved you as much as if you were his own. Course you didn't turn out like I expected but you're still mine. All I got in this world."

Carrie, sitting there over your coffee cup in a wasteland of worn-out silver wedding rings, feeding yourself confections of motherhood like the display cakes in the bakery where you worked— all trimming over cardboard. I fiddled with my cup and she went on, "You were born to be my baby. That's what Pastor Needle said and I raised you to be a lady. Did the best I could."

"I know, Mom. I'm grateful to you for taking care of me when I was tiny, feeding me, clothing me. You didn't have much to spare. I really am grateful."

"Don't thank me. That's what mothers are for. I wanted to do it."

I glanced up at the clock; ten minutes and my cab would be there. She watched me check the time and her eyes tightened. "When you coming back this way again?"

"Can't say. It's hard for me to get the money up."

"Now see, it don't make sense for you to want women. No woman's gonna keep you. You go out there and marry some man and he'll keep you. You'll have money then. You'll be sorry. There's no security with a woman."

"Hell, you married a man and you didn't have

money. And security—you're secure when you're dead."

"Such talk. I can't keep up with you. When's your cab coming?"

"In about ten minutes."

"Well, I said all I got to say. I packed you sandwiches and there's some Switzer cheese in wax paper. Buy yourself some milk and have a good lunch. There's three hard boiled eggs too so you don't have to buy any food. That's all your old mother can give you." Her eyes got wet again. "I done the best I could. Honey, I'm so sorry I ain't rich. I'd buy you a moviehouse of your own if I was. I don't say nothing this week but it hurts me to see you so drawn. You're too skinny, girl. You're up there working and working yourself. You always was a hard worker. I'm afraid you drive yourself too hard. Dammit to hell. I grow up with nothing and I want my kid to have something. You're starting out from scratch cause I got nothing to give you. I did the best I could. Don't hate me, honey, don't hate me."

I put my arms around her and her white head hid underneath my breasts. "Mom, I don't hate you. We're different people, strongwilled people. We don't always see eye to eye. That's why we fought so much. I don't hate you."

"And I never said that thing you said I said. I never said you weren't mine. You are mine."

"Oh, I got mixed up, that's all. Forget it."

"I love you. You're the only thing I keep living for. What else I got—the t.v."

"I love you too."

The taxi honked outside and Carrie looked as though she'd seen the angel of death. She tried to carry my suitcase, but I told her not to do that. I ran out with the equipment and came back for my suitcase. She stretched her hands toward me. "Give this old dried apricot a kiss." I gave her a hug and a kiss and as I turned to go to the taxi she coughed, "You write me, now. You write me, you hear?"

I turned and nodded that I would. I couldn't speak. The taxi pulled away and Carrie was leaning against the faded pink wall waving goodbye. I waved back.

Carrie, Carrie whose politics are to the right of Genghis Khan. Who believes that if the good Lord wanted us to live together he'd have made us all one color. Who believes a woman is only as good as the man she's with. And I love her. Even when I hated her, I loved her. Maybe all kids love their mothers, and she's the only mother I've ever known. Or maybe underneath her crabshell of prejudice and fear there's a human being that's loving. I don't know but either way I love her.

Professor Walgren's scrotum shriveled when I walked back in with the equipment. He raved on about how irresponsible I was to go off with all that hardware when other people needed to use it. He threatened to revoke my scholarships but had to back off from that idea since it was my last semester and the semester was nearly over. He sputtered, fumed, blew his nose, and eventually shut up.

Project night was a big event. All the other students had their "chicks" with them vying for who was best dressed in the downwardly-mobile category. They introduced their dates as "my chick" or "my old lady." I came by myself. It freaked them out that I didn't swish in with some bearded number sporting a tie-dyed tee shirt. And the projects began. The one that drew the most applause was a gang rape on an imaginary

Martian landscape with half the cast dressed as Martians, the other half, as humans. All the men mumbled about what a profound racial statement it was. The "chicks" gasped.

My film was last on the list and by the time we got to it some of the audience had already left. There was Carrie speeding away in her rocking chair looking straight at the camera and being herself. No quick cuts to steals from Kenneth Anger, no tinfoil balls dropping out of the sky to represent nuclear hail—just Carrie talking about her life, the world today, and the price of meat. I had edited it as best I could. It fluttered here and there but it was twenty minutes of her life, her life as she saw it and relived it for the camera. The last thing she said in the film was, "I'm gonna turn this house into a big gingerbread cake with icing on the corners. Then when those goddamn bill collectors come after me I just tell 'em to break off a piece of the house and leave me alone. In time they eat the whole house," she chuckled, "then I'll be sittin' out in the sunshine that the good Lord made. I'll be out in the lilies of the field that's richer than all King Solomon's gold. That ain't a bad way to die when yer as old as I am." She laughed a strong, certain laugh and as that laugh died so did the light.

No one clapped. No one made a sound. I began rewinding the film and they filed out by the projection table. I looked at these cohorts of mine through the last years and not one of them could look me in the face. They walked out of the room silently and the last one to go was Professor Walgren. He stopped at the door, turned to say something, thought the better of it; his eyes on the floor, he slowly shut the door so that it didn't make a sound.

I graduated *summa cum laude* and Phi Beta Kappa. I didn't go to the ceremony, they sent me my diploma in the mail. I didn't go back to the department to lord it over the undergraduates. After my showing I took my cans of film plus the Arriflex as reparations and tried to get a job. M-G-M asked me to start as a secretary. Warner Brothers Seven Arts was interested in my publishing skills and offered me one fifty a week to start if I'd work grinding out PR for their latest releases. My technical skills were very impressive to them. They were sure it would help when I wrote press copy for their latest Warren Beatty flick.

The underground filmmakers were more direct. One famous man asked me if I'd consider dressing as a hermaphrodite for his next film. He adored my face and thought I'd be too, too divine as the boy-girl, girl-boy in his next naked take-off of Shakespeare. Said he'd make me a star. Young and Rubicam told me that I'd have to start as a secretary but in a few years I'd get to shoot commercials. Wells, Rich, Green told me the same thing, but they offered me more money and a better office. The guy who made the Martian rape went right into CBS as an assistant director for a children's program. CBS was full up, they told me.

No, I wasn't surprised, but it still brought me down. I kept hoping against hope that I'd be the bright exception, the talented token that smashed sex and class barriers. Hurrah for her. After all, I was the best in my class, didn't that count for something? I spent those bitter days (after squandering my lunch hour on job interviews) sitting in the office while Stella came in with story after story of Mr. Cohen's prostate problems, bitter days while I edited the *Compendium of Crafts* and thought I'd fracture along with the fifteen easy steps to facet glass. My bitterness was reflected in the news, full of stories about people my own age raging down the streets in protest. But somehow I knew my rage wasn't their rage and they'd have run me out of their movement for being a lesbian anyway. I read somewhere too that women's groups were starting but they'd trash me just the same. What the hell. I wished I could be that frog back at Ep's old pond. I wished I could get up in the morning and look at the day the way I used to when I was a child. I wished I could walk down the streets and not hear those constant, abrasive sounds from the mouths of the opposite sex. Damn, I wished the world would let me be myself. But I knew better on all counts. I wish I could make my films. That wish I can work for. One way or another I'll make those movies and I don't feel like having to fight until I'm fifty. But if it does take that long then watch out world because I'm going to be the hottest fifty-year-old this side of the Mississippi.

ABOUT THE AUTHOR

RITA MAE BROWN is the bestselling author of *Rubyfruit Jungle, In Her Day, Six of One, Southern Discomfort, Sudden Death, High Hearts, Bingo, Starting from Scratch: A Different Kind of Writers' Manual, Venus Envy, Dolley: A Novel of Dolley Madison in Love and War, Riding Shotgun,* and *Rita Will: Memoir of a Literary Rabble-Rouser.* With her tiger cat, Sneaky Pie, she also collaborates on the Mrs. Murphy mystery series, including *Wish You Were Here; Rest in Pieces; Murder at Monticello; Pay Dirt; Murder, She Meowed;* and *Murder on the Prowl.* An Emmy-nominated screenwriter and a poet, she lives in Charlottesville, Virginia.

RITA MAE

BROWN

___56497-8	**VENUS ENVY**	$6.50/$8.99 in Canada
___28220-4	**BINGO**	$6.50/$8.99
___27888-6	**HIGH HEARTS**	$6.50/$8.99
___27573-9	**IN HER DAY**	$6.50/$8.99
___27886-X	**RUBYFRUIT JUNGLE**	$6.99/$9.99
___27446-5	**SOUTHERN DISCOMFORT**	$6.50/$8.99
___26930-5	**SUDDEN DEATH**	$6.50/$8.99
___27887-8	**SIX OF ONE**	$6.99/$9.99
___57224-5	**RIDING SHOTGUN**	$6.50/$8.99
___56949-X	**DOLLEY:**	$6.50/$8.99

A NOVEL OF DOLLEY MADISON IN LOVE AND WAR

___34630-X   **STARTING FROM SCRATCH:** $12.95/$17.95

A DIFFERENT KIND OF WRITER'S MANUAL
